Journeying Up The Mountain WITH THE Tantric Goddesses

An Initiation into the Ten Cosmic Powers

RUTH DAVIS

iUniverse®

JOURNEYING UP THE MOUNTAIN WITH
THE TANTRIC GODDESSES
AN INITIATION INTO THE TEN COSMIC POWERS

iUniverse books may be ordered through booksellers or by contacting:

iUniverse
1663 Liberty Drive
Bloomington, IN 47403
www.iuniverse.com
844-349-9409

ISBN: 978-1-6632-4889-3 (sc)
ISBN: 978-1-6632-4890-9 (e)

Library of Congress Control Number: 2022922801

Print information available on the last page.

iUniverse rev. date: 12/12/2022

CONTENTS

PREFACE
by da Sanda Wadi

Ruth's surprising sojourn into the adventures of the spirit is a wild and intoxicating initiation. I was spirited along as if I were there to receive the teachings, with no separation, totally a part of the proceedings as they unfolded. They reminded me so much of my time in Burma as a Buddhist nun. I ordained, shaved my head, and wore robes and then spent 15 years traveling back and forth to the remote monastery to partake fully in Burmese monastic life. Everything was so new to me and I was so receptive to the spiritual world unfolding before me, trusting fully in the strange and mysterious way the teachings were transmitted. One of the strangest tenets was the belief in the 31 realms of existence. I had no grounding for this but was fascinated by the purity of the teachings and the stories of the sublime upper realm beings. This captivating experience was brought to mind again on the journey Ruth takes us on. It is such a pure and sublime journey, there is not any other explanation than that of the upper realms, and the veil between the worlds being made manifest. Although I am unfamiliar with Indian cosmology, the divine feminine that she presents so fully and clearly, is indeed a deep receptive teaching that touches the core of our being and is a healing potion for our times.

FOREWORD

Life is an exquisite tapestry made of the colors and textures of our experiences. Seeing the threads of our being woven into an amazing and intricate pattern, we wonder how much we weave and how much is woven for us.

At six years old I began taking ballet. In ballet we practice at the bar, strengthening our muscles and refining the precision of our movement. At the end of class we take what we have learned to the open space of the dance floor. The moment I raised my arms above my head I felt my heart lifting up to the sky and to God. Realizing I was dancing to God, the experience of joy was overwhelming. I felt the warmth of the love through my whole body and the pure ecstasy that was present in the moment. I was dancing to God, in God, with God and it was all inside of me and outside of me. I thought all the dancers were having the same experience. Looking back I realize this was my first experience of being inside my heart, my Spiritual Heart, my soul.

At 16 I began a devotional Indian path with the primary focus being meditation. Indian mysticism and vedic wisdom captured all the answers I sought concerning the purpose of life. Years later I discovered being inside my heart while dancing was identical to meditation. For it is in meditation that we enter the Spiritual Heart and experience Self-Realization, the Light of Christ, or our Buddha nature, the emanation of God's love keeping everything alive. This understanding became the foundation for how I teach Heartfulness meditation.

Having a natural inclination for the metaphysical, I deepened into mystic Catholicism as well and moved to Assisi, Italy. I became both a devotee of Mother Mary of the West and Durga from the East. My husband and I built three silent retreat centers, two in Assisi and one in Northern California.

During a one-year practice to God as Mother, while still living in Assisi, I uncovered the ten cosmic powers, the goddesses that emanate from Durga. They revealed themselves through dance, one movement at a time, expressing their essence and influence in my daily life.

Finally having a way to express the deepest meaning of movement, I shared the movement practice with our retreat participants as a natural extension of meditation. I wrote about the underlying philosophy driving the dance in my first book, Sacred Movement Ritual. A year-long practice to the Divine Mother emerged, which I shared with many students.

Fifteen years later in February of 2020, "Journeying up the Mountain" began to pour through me like a Bollywood movie in full animation, with an aliveness that was unstoppable. Each of my meditation periods were overflowing with images, words, meanings, and goddesses. My Divine Mother practice starts each year on the new moon of March, was rapidly approaching. I hurriedly invited a mature group of friends and students together. Having practiced with me before, they jumped right in. As the chapters came pouring through me, I wrote them down and read them aloud to everyone. One chapter on each new moon was read, invoking one mother one month at a time. The story unfolded in front of us all. I myself did not know the outcome, it was in Mothers hands.

On the new moon of August 2020, I read aloud to my students the latest chapter that invoked the presence of Kali. Five hours later our retreat center and home in Northern California got caught in a wildfire along with 210 other homes and burned to the ground. This book is among the few things I carried out that fateful night. Trusting the goddesses were guiding the journey, my husband and I, along with family and community members, came back to the ruins two days later. We all felt a peace that was unmistakable. It was as if the Retreat Center had lifted up and expanded into the universe. All of the love that had been cultivated there could no longer be contained to one spot on Earth. Her love spread out into everyone and everything. One statue survived, the statue of St Francis. Burning for hours he stood through it all. With his copper color blackened, his naked humility was pure gold.

Everything was gone. However, we distinctly felt that the true gift of the Retreat Center remained. It was the present in the silence, present in the love from the community praying for us. The world can change but love and peace are preserved in the expanded body of silence we share.

Miraculously the book kept manifesting into words and I continued to write. The last four Mothers, four chapters, were completed in between moving, exhausting insurance drama, and overwhelming paperwork. Writing became sailing; with my heart as my rudder, trust in my sails, Mother God was my boat. Together we managed to weather the storm of life. I offer this book to you as it appeared to us all spontaneously.

INTRODUCTION

Journeying up the mountain with the Tantric Goddesses is the story of the incarnate soul traveling back to God, the Source. It is written through metaphors in a casual, unassuming, even playful way. It is based on devotion to the Divine Mother and specifically that of Durga. Devotion means we step into the Mother's love, into Her heart, where we feel alive. She is all around us and moving through us. We are stepping into aliveness itself.

Durga's purpose is to conquer the mind, our sense of separateness, by finding 10 wisdom forms, goddesses, cosmic powers, inside herself. She reveals them to her students, in this case, one chapter at a time through daily activities, initiations, and meditations. The Beings assist our every moment, influencing and refining our soul's progression. In each chapter the environment shifts according to the influence of the different Mother or goddess that is present, presiding over the environment.

Historically, Indian masters used an internal path of meditation as the research method, a path to go back to God to understand the purpose of life, the highest meaning of being incarnated. In so doing, they heal or dissolve the karma (our human conditioning influencing the mind) which keeps the soul on the wheel of birth and death. Once the karma is resolved, the mind healed, the soul can be released from this cycle and merge back to God.

The journey up the mountain is metaphorical. We are traveling the mountain of our incarnation back to God where all answers Are. In so doing we elevate this life and future lifetimes (if any) to the highest version of an incarnate being, one that is free, full of the Light, and at peace with all that is.

The story is the Path to Liberation, enlightenment, Self Realization, Moksha, merging with the One. It is the path of the immortal being. Mystics from all traditions search for this One as their Source for the illumination of their Soul. As we do it for ourselves we do it for the All, as we are not separate.

CHAPTER ONE

JOURNEY OF OUR SOUL

We find ourselves standing at the base of a sacred mountain. As our eyes travel up her massive form of hills, peaks and craggy edges, clouds and fog surrounding her, create visions of realms to travel through. Now and again we catch glimpses of distant waterfalls and forests. The open sky above her makes our hearts leap with joy. We gasp and swiftly breath in her fresh reality, as enlivened air, that fills our lungs with the overwhelming beauty of all of creation. It is as if we are being born and taking our first breath.

Immediately we sense we are called to travel up to her highest peaks. This is not any ordinary mountain but rather a holy mountain that will guide the journey of our Soul. Somehow we know our travels will reveal the meaning and purpose of this life and notice we are not alone but that there are others walking with us and we are traveling up the mountain together.

Our hearts have been called to the highest mountain, the highest in the known universe. We have all been called to seek the highest peak, the highest wisdom. Something inside our hearts said Yes.

Quieting into that yes has put us on the path. It was a yes to Her love, the love of the Divine Mother, Mother God, the Source of everything created. Our yes reveals the karmic readiness of the Soul. With that, we are suddenly prepared even though we carry no outward supplies. Yet inwardly, we feel we have everything we need.

The Journey

Each one of us walks up the mountain from our place in the world. Some of us are traveling together, some seemingly alone. Everyone has their own personal relationship with the Mother. We know the answers await us at the top of the mountain no matter what we seek.

As we climb we don't really see each other. A deep cloud descends over the mountain calming the outer pull or noise of the physical world we are leaving and softens the anxiety in the mind. We sense a powerful presence accompanying us.

At first the journey seems daunting as we are only walking. Insecurity arises and in response our inner knowing comes forward.

"Have no fear, the journey will take nine days." This inner knowing is as spoken from our heart and yet from the presence all around us.

"Nine days?" someone responds out loud worriedly. Yet all of us know this is true when we hear it.

"But what about provisions?" someone else puts forward. Again, as soon as the question arises it is answered from the voice of Knowingness, "There will be enough and all personal needs will be met along the way," it responds comfortingly.

A quelling of questions occurs like we finally drank enough water. The only preparation needed was the dedication to yes and the upward joy that arose in our body as a commitment to that yes. And we set out.

Obscuring our vision, the deep cloud has lowered into fog and the surroundings seem more harsh and ominous. Our feet touch some prickly leaves. Looking down we realize we are not wearing shoes.

"This seems odd," our awareness declares. "For such a long journey?"

The road begins to narrow and an old woman appears on the side begging. Some of us give her whatever we have, others of us try to avoid her. She will be the last person we see and we realize it is only our human fear that can trick us away from ascending the mountain. And again we see that all our queries, darkness or discomfort are only our fears appearing in front of us.

At this realization the cloud of our delusions begins to lift. We are leaving the cities behind, the sounds lessen, and the vast nature spreads out before us welcoming us further. The shadowy nature of the physical realm disappears as we enter a different part of the journey.

The Forest

The sun is now rising and is at high noon, in its full radiance. The road leads us into a lush forest. Here the cool air greets and there is an awakening to the abundance that is present. Moist air, soft ground, warm sunlight filters through the trees. We realize we have entered a higher realm. One of us turns to us all as a light ray touches his heart. His eyes say,

"The sunlight is healing every corner of my heart's longing. It is like holes of disappointment are being filled with love and being healed by it" as tears stream down his face.

And with that the sunlight pours its rays onto each one of us communicating,

"This warmth is the Yes put forth from your innermost heart."

We realize love is a grand concert being played by the orchestra of nature around us. The forest trees and streams, birds and animals compose the sound of love that greets us. Somehow our awareness knows we are only passing through this realm. We don't want to leave it; but our inner knowing is guiding us onward to something greater.

Beyond happiness we notice the ground is soft under our feet and we have no need to eat. Any worry has completely vanished in the abundance of this great forest. The smell of berries and flowers satiate us with happiness. We instinctively hold our hand on our heart in order to absorb the presence we are engaged with.

Looking down at our bodies we realize some of us have tattered clothes, others sweet dresses or shirts, still others are completely naked. This seems to be some sort of previous conditioning of our mind that is left over from earthly life. The inner knowing comes forth again,

"All of us are simply human, do not judge each other." it explains. Encouraging us onward it continues,

"Come, you have so much farther to go. This is only the Astral realm."

Occasionally a monkey appears and hurriedly runs out in front of us. At some point we realize we are following him and he is leading us perfectly.

The mountain way turns as we reach a clearing where the trees have stopped growing. We sense our awareness expanding to match the open plain. Far up ahead it appears the top of the mountain is within reach.

The Sunrise

It has turned to night time and the sky is packed with stars. The moon is in its last quarter providing little light, but the stars are enough. We keep walking, the journey is effortless now. Far up ahead the monkey runs beyond our sight. We are not sure we will ever find him again. Our eyes adjust to the dense star packed sky as it calls us forward. The air is cool but we are never cold. The deep sky touches the depth of our soul, inviting us farther up the mountain, farther into our heart.

The sky wraps its arms around us holding our hearts in stillness. The deepening quiet pulls us closer to itself as if to say,

"Move into the quiet of your heart where all peace exists." Our knowing comes forward to say, "To be this high up on the mountain we must have been walking for about six days."

As the morning greets us the sunrise turns everything pink. As the sun rises it rises in our hearts. Everything happening outwardly is happening in our heart. There is a slight layer of clouds across the horizon that make the sunrise more intense and this light penetrates our soul. Our awareness observes,

"Is it speaking to us, teaching us ?"

The Precipice

We feel we are on our last day of walking. Our energy becomes as light as a feather and we can almost float the rest of the way. Up ahead the monkey appears again and as we see him we are transported to him. That's a change. It seems we are traveling without a physical body now, traveling only in spirit. Our knowing responds with,

"Yes."

We move in the direction of the highest peak we can see, when the path gently guides us to a cliffside plateau off to the right. As we walk towards the cliff area we see the others gathering that are on the journey with us. They have traveled from all over the world to be here. Some have already arrived and are sitting looking out meditating on the sunrise. We all seem to know what to do and without speaking sit down to join in.

Our perception heightened, we notice we are much younger now, with vibrant hair and skin. Our clothes have become simple white veils of silk. Our feet love the packed earth, they are never cold or sore but feel soft and supple.

We realize after some time that everyone has arrived and this stirs our heart with happiness. No one is missing or alone. We do not need to talk, we all understand each other perfectly, communicating with each other through a transfer of knowledge, a transfer of energy.

"Telepathy," the inner knowing observes.

Slowing down we realize it is a time to simply sit and take in the sunrise. We close our eyes as if to sleep. But when we open our eyes again it has been two days and the sun is still a sunrise and we realize this is the way it will be here. These days are necessary for our spirits to adjust to this new realm.

We sit for days and nights, the monkey dancing between us brings us fruit and flowers while the sunrise teaches us. The sunrise teaches us about the pure potential hidden in our hearts, and our innocence woven through the silk cloth that covers our nakedness.

Our inner knowing awakens us,

"This is the presence of Mother Dhumavati. She will be the first Mother you encounter." She is not appearing to us as a being but rather as the experience we are having. And we sense now that she was also the presence in the clouds as we ascended the mountain.

She is the stillness and quiet found in the continuous sunrise, the pure potential found in the emptying of our minds as we let go of the external world. Her vast openness welcomes every part of us as we transition from our earthly life to internal realms of the heart, our soul. She is also the transition itself.

As Her energy speaks a mist appears around us that seems to be carrying her voice,

"You have entered the Causal Realm, the realm of the goddesses, the MahaVidyas (wisdom mothers). Here the highest, most refined beings live, teach and inform your lives and practices. We are all different aspects of Mother God, the Divine Mother herself," she continues.

Here, in this realm, we can breathe freely. There are no stuck emotions. There is a freshness in the air. As we become aware of it, snow begins to fall. It is as if the mist has transformed itself into snow and the snow is felt as grace descending upon us. It soaks gently into our body, into our skin, muscles, bones and nerves. The healing of the Mother's energy is penetrating everything.

Mother Dhumavati is healing every corner of our human trials and sorrows as well. And as Her love settles to the ground the earth springs forth little flowers. Grace is everywhere, soaked into everything. She is giving us her gifts because we persevered and listened. We said yes, trusted, and did not turn back. She has calmed the earth of our soul, the ground of our being, to give us everything. And the monkey just dances.

The voice of Knowingness whispers,

"This is where we will gather day after day, on the edge of the mountain, the precipice, to learn from the sunrise, from Mother Dhumavati."

CHAPTER TWO

WOMB OF GOD

The Seeds

Sitting on the precipice a large white owl swoops down over our heads. Her wings tell us this descent into the quiet was necessary to prepare us for the journey of our Soul.

With the calm of the morning sunrise, soft on our eyes we feel a touch on our shoulder. We look up but no one's there. Someone has left a bowl with little folded paper packets inside. We each take one knowing they were meant for us. I am the last one to take an envelope and I realize there are two, one extra. Looking around I see indeed everyone has theirs. Knowing this must be a special gift, I take the larger of the two feeling my greed and my hiding.

As we open the folded paper we see it has been inscribed with a language we do not understand, but we know intuitively it is a continuous prayer or mantra. We feel the love in the words as we touch them. As we unwrap them further we discover seeds inside. They are amazing, some are gold, some of every color, some are black. Someone has left us an amazing treasure.

We all hear inside ourselves,

"Take very close care of these. These are very important. Put them somewhere safe." As we try to figure out where that might be, a shiny black crow swoops down tauntingly, threatening to pick them away,

"Keep them safe!" she cackles. The monkey jumps up at her and bats her away.

The Cabin

As the air warms we start to stand and the monkey sitting with us runs over to the bushes. We know now to watch him closely. Suddenly we realize there is a tiny little cabin there among the bushes. It's been here all along or so it seems. We did not see it yesterday. But here it is in plain sight. It is a tiny little cabin with one window and one door. There is smoke coming out of the chimney and we look at each other in amazement. Someone is living way up here? How can that be? The scene is so inviting and sweet and we instantly know the teacher lives here.

Someone has been tending the flowers all around it and a glow comes from inside inviting us closer. As we approach, suddenly two young women appear and stop us from going inside. They guide us to the side of the house instead. Here they have prepared hot water and herbs to bathe us in. They lovingly take us and wash our feet. We are so absorbed in the tenderness of their work on our feet, that we realize only later they have washed our entire body. There are herbs still stuck to our skin here and there as they re-robe us. And the smell is intoxicating. They have cleared karmas and samskaras of all kinds in order for us to enter the hut.

Now they tell us, always without words, that we can go inside. But first they hand us a pouch for our seed packets and separately they give us flowers and herbs as an offering to take with us.

In Awe

As we all group up at the front door we realize how large we are. The door is much smaller than a normal door, seemingly made for a much smaller person. And we also realize there is no way we are all going to fit inside this tiny little cabin. And as we notice this, we recognize it is our human conditioning, our ego that is too large to enter. But the girls open the door anyway, giving us permission, and with that we move inside... as we move in, the room enlarges to fit us. Suddenly we all have plenty of room. It is like the experience of a womb expanding. The Mother expands, creates room, to include, welcoming us all.

They indicate for us to sit on the floor. Our senses are taking in overwhelming sights and smells of pungent herbs hanging on the walls and off strings above our heads. An occasional honey bee sniffs the hanging herbs. The smell fills our nose and lungs, some of us sneeze. This smell is healing in and of itself.

The young women tend to the fire in the fireplace. A copper pot is nestled just above the flame and we know instinctively that the fire and pot are always going. The cabin, very simple, holds one table, one chair, a prep area for the herbs with a short stool, small hand woven colorful rugs here and there.

One girl, the youngest maybe 12 or 13, has long warm blond braided hair, which seems out of place. Impeccably dressed, she wears little colored fabric shoes. This is unusual because everyone knows here you travel easier if you are not wearing shoes. Shoes indicate a heavier layer of unresolved karma.

She seems to be in charge of the herbs and keeping everything immaculate. And suddenly in my heart I realize she is going to be one of my best friends. I hear her name but I cannot repeat it yet, as the language is too foreign. And the other young woman is maybe seven years older with dark skin and black braided hair and seems to be in charge of greeting and organizing. She's absorbed writing everything down while we wait, for what we do not know.

It is rather dark inside with only one candle and the fire going. We now notice a second window behind the prep area. The safety inside this room is palpable and we know somehow this little cabin has been and will be here throughout time, without changing. We continue to wait patiently.

The Teacher

Then as if on cue both the young women turn and go to their knees as they hear a small door open on the side of the room. Low down on the ground an old brown skinned woman appears, she has long black braided hair, and is wearing the typical attire of this region—a long dress with pants underneath. Her stature belies the enormity of her energy and we are overpowered by her love. Her legs are bent permanently in a cross-legged position, "from continuous hours of meditation" the young women communicate to us through their eyes.

She rises only partly, only enough to move shuffle forward on the outside edges of her feet. The young women motion us to offer our flowers and we inch closer to lay them at her feet. The young women have taught us to always bring an offering of whatever we have as a way to receive the blessings of our time here. They arrange them to be closer to her.

Our hearts are overwhelmed by her attention noticing she came out only to greet us. The room has increased in size creating space for everyone. With tears flowing down our faces, noses running, someone brings us handkerchiefs. The younger girl hands the old woman a bowl. As she reaches for it, a glistening object catches our eyes from the bosom of her dress. We see a small golden key pinned to her blouse over her heart. She raises the bowl filled with warm porridge stirred with butter, sprinkled with cinnamon and bits of fruit. She motions us to come closer so she can feed us directly from her fingers.

We suddenly realize we are starving and that she loves us completely. We eat like babies until we cannot eat anymore. The young women attending her wipe her hands as she feeds us. The taste is amazing, warm, and sweet and every part of us wants as much as she is willing to give us. She feeds us until we can take no more. The girls use telepathy once again,

"She is feeding you from the highest realm of Light, pure spirit, where she lives inside constantly."

And we know this is not ordinary food but rather the Light of God-as-Mother made into food. The golden key glistens in the fire light and we lay down to fall fast asleep.

The Cave

Awakening the next day under the trees surrounding the cabin, we gather our senses. The young girls busy with more preparations for us are piling wood into a small bread oven. Realizing their work is intended to care only for us we are touched all over again. Humbled it strikes us how our every need, on every level, is lovingly taken care of. There is an inner accepting of our small selves. How can we be worthy of such love?

It seems they knew we were coming; they have been planning for us. But suddenly we realize how implausible this situation is. Where are they getting everything? Is someone bringing in supplies? We know now, somehow, that the nearest village is three days away by walking. And if you have shoes on, it takes even longer. But somehow they have everything they need and everything we need. Nature seems to be expanding to meet the needs of everyone.

We let go of thinking as the young women direct us over to the mouth of a cave. Approaching the cave the monkey sprints ahead, his movements startling a snake that has been protecting the entrance.

The monkey's energy tells it,

"I will do that now." And she moves away.

The monkey seems to be evolving as well. He is able to use his energy to communicate and is taking personal responsibility for us. The cave has a wide opening like loving arms greeting us. Finding places to sit, we accommodate each other as we nestle into the heart of the cave.

The Rainbow Phenomenon

We are drawn into meditation naturally with no sense of time. Our attention is being drawn into the center of our hearts that is glowing, radiant, and growing into a massive sun. Our inner knowing tells us,

"This pull into the center of our heart is the teacher anchoring our awareness in Pure Light, Pure Spirit."

The inner world of our hearts has expanded beyond the walls even as we sit in the safety of the cave. Our minds settle deeper into acceptance. We know this radiance and this cave are always our home. We never need to search further than this.

Suddenly, in what could only be deemed a cosmic event, there is a turmoil of weather in the upper sky in front of us. A giant sun appears, way too large to be a sun of this universe.

To our amazement the eternal sunrise of this realm remains the same in the middle of the sky. As we peer over the precipice we can see into the distance below. Clouds, rain, lightning, storms of all kinds are looming over the cities of life on earth.

Lifting our heads back to the amazing site of the giant sun, it suddenly sprays forth a rainbow light of 10 colors. This event covers the entire upper sky. The rainbow keeps moving out, spreading out, and suddenly turns heading for our cave. Its colors run all over the cave walls carving its light into them, when suddenly it pulls together into a narrow pillar or ribbon of rainbow light. This light then enters the top of our heads, weaves all the way down through our body, heart, chakras and nadis, sushumna only to travel all the way back up and out withdrawing itself back into the giant sun which then just as quickly as it came—disappears.

The teacher's silent guidance echoing through the cave explains these are the etheric vibrations of the ten wisdom mothers, and that all the energy in our body has been transformed to rainbow light, their essence. All senses and spiritual vibrations are being aligned with the pure radiant spirit of the Great Heart in our own heart.

Plunged into a deep peace, there remains only a pink light like a fog throughout the cave. This peace is the one constant, true reality; all is this Light, this vast open love. All is this peace.

Inner Preparation

Knowing we need to integrate the experience of the ten colors we fall fast asleep. Inwardly we are preparing to receive the energies and wisdom of the ten Mothers, the MahaVidyas.

Ten days and nights pass and we awaken only because of a delicious scent of fresh bread billowing through the cave. It has been left at the mouth of the cave laden with flowers set on a golden platter. As we form a circle around it a large white owl appears calling, "Who, who, who." It is telling us that by sharing this bread, ingesting it deep into our souls, the wisdom of all the ages is being imparted.

Eating slowly, thoughtfully, we let each morsel dissolve completely in our mouth before swallowing and taking another. We make sure everyone has an equal amount. The taste is so satisfying we need not eat now for

30 days until the next new moon. We are in the gestation period of Light becoming our true body.

We have been shown the unending love of Mother Bhuvaneshwari, the nurturer, the Womb of God. She has prepared the pure Light of Mothers love in the cave of Her heart. As we close our eyes, the rainbow light carries us into sleep and we rest.

CHAPTER THREE

MOTHERS ARMS

Pondering

Several of us lay down near the edge of the precipice together staring upward and enjoying the colorful sky. The enormous sunrise fills us with a tender gentleness and the slow beginning of a new day. Here that means we get to explore the workings of the universe while being protected by love.

We watch clouds floating across the sky, dancing in their growing, dispersing and reshaping into whatever form they wish. Someone says,

"Look, the sky and clouds are teaching us." "Yes," someone else says.

Our inner knowing comes forward,

"The interplay of the clouds and the sky teach us of those things that change and that which is unchanging. The clouds change free in their formlessness. Whereas the nature of the sky is steady, present and alive."

We begin to ponder this relationship and how it fits in with our own experience. We begin to ask each other questions,

"What is changing? What is remaining the same? And that which is changing, can it change without holding on, being like a cloud?"

Without doubt we realize the clouds are teaching us about emotions and how we hold onto the past or to worries of the future. We do not move and give in like clouds.

"Yes," someone says responding out loud,

"I get very stuck in my position of frustration, anger or disappointment."

We all agree that much of our human struggle is based on where we cannot move inside. The sky answers back,

"Allow your emotions to move like the cloud and then you can feel the freedom I am offering."

We emerge from our pondering to the youngest girl bringing us tea. It is very bitter and we wonder why. But she indicates it is medicinal and we trust.

We hear her name for the first time as if a tree spoke it, "Nirmala Devi."

This realm is the teaching, opening our minds and hearts. We are learning from whatever catches our attention. And it is meant to catch our attention so we can learn from it and ponder the true reality. We realize the realm and everything in it is speaking to us through everything we connect with, whether it be a tree, animal, clouds, or the sky.

As I look toward Nirmala Devi, I see she is wearing a beautiful golden bracelet with diamonds and two hearts intertwined. She feels my question as if I had touched her. She lovingly touches it and raises her eyes to meet mine,

"From my family," she responds.

Suddenly, we all begin to feel the effects of the tea. As we look at each other our eyes light up. As we reach out to touch our surroundings it is as if the universe has opened. For a moment nothing has real borders and every object becomes iridescent.

The tea seems to have washed away some type of crust or mental conditioning, around our nervous system preventing our ability to see, to experience the underlying radiance that all of creation is built from. We sit with the tea and our softened experience for several hours as the worldly objects slowly take form once again. But amazingly they retain a glow that speaks to their underlying cosmic beauty.

Curiosity & Creativity

Curiosity has welled up in almost everyone and we begin to explore our surroundings. One of us picks herbs and studies the plants, talking to

Nirmala Devi. She teaches her about the Devis of each plant. Others have gone deeper into the cave. Unbridled in our excitement we listen to each other's discoveries,

"I found a deep clear bubbling reservoir," someone says.

"And I found walls dripping something like honey," someone else chimes in, adding,

"It's all in underground caverns, among the stalactites and stalagmites." Someone else adds,

"And I saw the older girl tending white cows in the forest, with a baby white elephant following her around."

Someone else exclaims,

"Well, I found a doorway to a different realm inside a cluster of trees where you can get down to a river; it's amazing."

I have captured time with Nirmala Devi to find out what she is all about. She is so close in my heart I just need time with her. She beckons me into the forest and I lose track of her. And then I hear the most amazing music being played, that seems to be carried on the rays of light filtering through the trees. It is a piano playing the most amazing concerts. I move towards the sound and there sits Nirmala devi playing a grand piano surrounded by mosses and ferns of all kinds.

"I am playing their music," she says.

And I begin to dance. I dance like I am 16 and on point as a ballet dancer. Her music lifts my body and allows me to leap through the air. Every imaginable position is attained and perfected by *her* precision on the keyboard. Our experience is intertwined, the music moving the dancer and the dancer shaping the music. But alas I cannot dance as long as she can play and I lay down in the leaves continuing to watch the trees dance to the music. I look back over and realize there is no piano at all but rather she is playing the leaves and branches around her. She knows me more than I know myself. She has created the piano and the music just for me.

I distinctly know she is not only my best friend but everyone's because here what happens to one happens to all. When you enter the forest with Nirmala Devi, she will give you the experience of your happiest self and your most creative self. Here in my understanding I see that she will, or maybe she already has shared this with each one of us, whether we paint, or write, sing, or teach. She is showing us the path of the highest sound which emerges from the Realm of Pure Light. It flows throughout the universe and supports each of us to create the purest form of sharing on earth. It appears as our natural talent.

A breeze whispers,

"You are witnessing the pure sound created by the Light. Your voice, your actions, your love will now be filled with this vibration and you will be consciously aware of it."

I find myself heading back to the cabin excited to find the others, heavenly exhausted from dancing in pure bliss.

Seeing

At the door of the cabin the older girl, Anam Cara, has collected pails of milk from the white cows to make butter. Our psychic hearing has increased which reveals her name. The baby white elephant playing alongside bumps into one of the pails spilling the milk everywhere. She immediately explores the pail with her trunk in hopes to get a drink of it.

I move around them to go inside. Everyone has been here for hours studying with Ammaji, the teacher, as her name appears as well. Her name pulls our heart. She has collected everyone around her, querying us about our experience of the clouds and sky.

"Yes, you are right," she says.

"You have done well to feel how the clouds can shift, change, disappear. They are formations in the mind, disturbances and impressions of all kinds from past lifetimes. They are karmas. The steady presence of the blue sky, the sky of the day, light, open and deep, peaceful, receptive *is the meditative mind*, pure mind, the higher self. In its true nature it does not hold fixed to any pattern or shape, but rather the *meditative mind* allows for the changing. In meditation you are dissolving the disturbances of the past and you are healing your karmas. Did you see the elephant?" she adds.

"Yes," we excitedly reply.

She nods and inwardly smiles, letting us know this is a good sign, implying our meditation is working and we are making progress. She slowly stirs a pot of butter and herbs while she talks with us.

A door has appeared at the back of the cabin where villagers have lined up. There was no door there before and I do not understand. Someone else realizing that I am also having the same question everyone else had tells me,

"If you go around the back of the cabin you won't see this door from the outside or any of the villagers, we already checked."

I sit down perplexed as I watch. The villagers have come for the herbs and treatments of Ammaji. They too have little shoes on. Some of them come inside and run over to her, running right through us, as if we are not there, and suddenly I realize they cannot see us. We can see them but they can't see us. It appears that those that arrive at this door are coming for physical ailments. That's why they are wearing shoes, they are living with heavier karma. Those that come through the front door are coming for spiritual ailments. But we are not sure our ailments are any less karmic.

The awareness that we cannot be seen makes us ponder; what can't we see? Are there other spirits in the room like us? When we are in the cave are there other spirits there like us? Are there any number of beings learning, hearing, and studying? Why can we only see the people we came with? Are they separate from us or do they represent parts of ourselves?

We realize the journey is much deeper than we expected and there is a plan that we are as yet unaware of.

We also realize there are different levels of seeing. The villagers could not see us but Ammaji and the girls could. Ammaji can see every being and is therefore teaching and working on different planes at once. What is her capacity? What capacity is needed? She asked us if we saw the baby elephant. Does that mean others cannot see her ?

Our pondering takes us back to the cave to meditate.

Compassion as a Thousand Arms

Walking back inside, I go to sit in my usual place when I notice someone is already there. This is odd because we have all found our own favorite spot. I am amazed that a part of me is actually annoyed at this and I go up to see who it is. I stop, frozen, as I notice it is Divine Mother Tara sitting there. I step back away and almost step on someone else who is sitting nearby. When I look down it is also Divine Mother Tara. I look around in amazement and realize everyone in the room is Tara, which can only mean I am too. As I run to find the only puddle of water that I know of in the cave and as I peer into it, yes indeed my reflection is Divine Mother Tara. I am overwhelmed with this experience and quiet myself to sit for meditation.

How can this be I wonder, my reflection is Her but my experience is me. Am I a reflection of her in some way? What teaching is she transmitting to me, to us? Does everyone have the same experience? As I sit with her impression deep in my psyche and soul she speaks,

"I am the seerer of all karma. I am there wherever, whenever you need to be carried. My hands and arms will catch you and guide you back to the Love."

And then yes, this teaching was present today in the cabin. I realize there are all levels of seeing. We have only touched the surface of this wisdom and the level of this compassion. And we hear Ammaji's voice,

"She is the Mother of compassion which is like milk being poured over the universe." And now we understand the baby elephant wanting the milk. The most innocent part of ourselves is the most precious and the Mother is constantly feeding it.

We meditate on seeing all with compassion, and seeing with no holding, so that change can be a freeing movement of joy across a limitless sky of being. We feel the inner dissolving of tensions or holdings from the soft healing balm of meditation. Our inner eyes are becoming clear. There are a thousand arms of Mother Tara holding every experience with love.

Under the night sky

The baby elephant has now found her way to the cave and the monkey jumps on her back and plays with her, pretending he is a great warrior.

We are overwhelmed by the vastness of love that is being shown; Ammaji with us and the villagers, the animals playing. Love can appear anywhere the attention *sees* it or goes to it. Love is transported to human experience by looking in its direction. And there is no limit to this seeing. Divine Mother Tara is carrying us, carrying everyone.

The baby elephant lies down in the middle of us and we all cuddle up to her and feel her breathing. She gazes at the night sky which has suddenly become very deep and welcoming. We follow her breathing and our own. They move together as one.

As we rise and fall on the rhythm of her breath we hear,

"Play in the sky of the night that is infinitely opening and eternal. The sky of the day, steady in peace, is the higher mind. But the sky of the night is eternity."

Again we rise and fall on her breath and we hear.

"The Great Heart is the sky of the night which is beyond the level of mind the sky of the day. Mind is but a filter, communicating between our experiences, the clouds, and the Great Heart breathing."

We feel the baby elephant's breath once again and on the rise and fall we hear,

"In meditation you are receiving your heart essence. This will wash and heal your mind, clearing all karmas. The clearer your mind, the more steady your heart, the more wisdom you hear from the Great Heart found in the night sky."

Laying here together on the precipice we experience the breath of the universe feeling its rhythm. The Great Heart lifts our spirits up out of our bodies and takes us up into the night sky and into Herself. We turn around looking back at our sweet circle on the ground, our physical bodies cuddling the baby elephant. We now know Her deep heart is our heart, our spirit. We are both on the ground looking up and in the sky looking down, inwardly and outwardly infinite. We are all lying in the breath of the universe. We are the breath of the universe.

CHAPTER FOUR

GIVING LOTUS

The Basket

Our amazing universe so vast in our hearts allows us to open in ways we never knew before. We realize the huge gift of everything that is already given. We start to experience each breath as a miracle to wonder over. Just stepping becomes magical. To feel the enormity of what is readily and generously given makes us aware of the magnitude of the abundance and beauty around us.

Anam Cara has joined us in our cave. She has brought with her a large basket, a pitcher of water, and starts to unpack. The mischievous monkey is anxious to find something to possess. She satisfies him right away with a bunch of small bananas that he grabs greedily, as if he will never get anymore ever, and runs off with his bounty to the trees.

Anam Cara carefully unpacks a large bowl and something wrapped in a delicate white cloth. Unfolding the cloth slowly she unveils a beautiful lotus plant. Filling the bowl with the water she motions us to come closer to form a circle around it. Very gently she places the lotus plant in the water.

"We are going to meditate on the lotus plant to bring forth it's flower, " she explains.

"Close your eyes." As we close our eyes, we feel the lotus plant immediately root itself in our muladhara. Anam Cara guides us,

"Open your eyes only slightly, just enough to see the lotus in the bowl. Now focus on the inner lotus that is traveling upward in your body, emerging from within."

As we do that the lotus in the bowl emerges and opens as well. It is spectacular in its beauty. Unlike any we have ever seen, with the most delicate white petals and green leaves and a deep pink center.

"Remain focused on the inner energy of the lotus," she continues.

With intention it moves slowly up our body following the length of our spine. A completed open lotus is left at each chakra along its way.

"This is the initiation into the richness of your inner beauty and abundance. Each chakra holds a different lotus and each lotus represents a different gift," she explains.

As the inner lotus reaches our heart, the lotus in the bowl slowly opens and a glittering light sparkles out from between its petals. The light arches out and touches each of our hearts simultaneously. We are enlivened to feel the opening of the universe itself and to the miracle of that which is constantly being given. As we receive the light from the outer lotus, our own heart lotus begins radiating as well. Anam Cara guides us,

"Allow the light to arch out from your heart, making a light bridge or arch to your loved ones hearts. Hold those in place. It does not matter if they are living or on the other side. And holding those light arches to your loved ones, now allow the light to arch out radiating light bridges to the hearts of each of your friends. Feel that and hold that in place as well. You are holding light arches to all your family and friends. And while still holding all of that in place, radiate light bridges to the hearts of everyone you have ever encountered. Holding all of that, now extend light bridges to everyone in the known universe."

At this point with bridges of lights radiating from around our heart, we are literally beaming. Our hearts are beaming ~ the opening of the universe ~ to everyone and everything. Our hearts are the source of love to the All. As this beaming continues the inner Lotus continues to travel upwards landing at our crown chakra. All Lotuses' in all chakras are now open, and very slowly and imperceptibly turning like the earth gracefully turning on its axis. They are complete in their ability to collect wisdom from the highest source. Cosmic wisdom is like gentle rain slowly falling from the highest realms. When the lotus' are open their petals collect it, absorbing it into their core. We revel in the sensation of being open and balanced on all levels, ready to receive, to drink all wisdom. We rest in meditation for hours taking walks and sitting on the precipice still feeling the gift of the open heart—open to the universe.

Siddhis as Treasure

Anam Cara comes and takes us on a walk. Our enlivened hearts feel everything we see and hear as alive. She stops at a spring. Here she picks up a rock in one hand and in the other a mountain appears, then she cups a handful of water and in the palm of her other hand the ocean appears, a small flame appears in one hand and the sun in the other. She is teaching us that everything is equal no matter how small or how large. The rock is as amazing as a mountain; a drop of water holds the ocean, the flame is the essence of the sun. And she says,

"Your spirit is equal to the All. God is your innermost nature."

She kneels down close to the spring and touching the ground nearby she directs the flow of the water into a basin of rocks appearing under her hand. The stream begins filling the basin. She says,

"See you can use the water to help others and the flow of water will keep filling up. And then you will have an endless supply of gifts. But if you use the water to impress…" and she snaps her fingers in the air in front of us, as if to impress us with her power,

"the flow of water will stop," she says. And then, sure enough, as she captured our awareness to her "power" the water stopped flowing.

"Use your gifts wisely," she encourages. "They are abundant but they can be curtailed by one's attitude."

Carefully she sets her hand on the ground. A loving light flows from her heart down her arm and into her hand. She has returned back to the energy of helping and the flow of water starts again which strengthens her new ability.

She tells us to be vigilant, to not be impressed with these new ways of being. They are quite natural here in this realm and a normal part of spiritual growth. These new ways of being are treasures and abilities, siddhis, not to be squandered, but rather they have deep spiritual meaning and purpose.

Anam Cara explains,

"These gifts can offer healing to the mind, body, soul and are a tangible treasure to be used to help others, which then will help us grow in *our* own spiritual progress."

We marvel in everything that is just given. We are a tiny part of an endless living universe and are one with *all of it*, all at the same time. And we suddenly realize that this is the realm of recognizing the treasure of what IS and what IS given. Humility & gratitude overtake us.

Heaven

We decide to explore the way down to the river that one of us found earlier, through the hidden passageway in the forest. The monkey psychically hears our request and starts to head for the forest. He knows exactly where to go and we begin to follow him. Today Anam Cara has been tasked by Ammaji to travel with us. The monkey senses the doorway and disappears into it.

We step through to follow him. And now we no longer exist in our forest, but rather we have entered into another realm. An expansive green valley with a path appears before us. Emerald green rolling hills, flowers, and pristine air greets us. Looking into the distance a vision of a milky white ocean appears with a river running down to it. Someone yells,

"Let's go!" Anam Cara, who is always extremely practical says,

"Wait. I will stay here holding the entryway so when you come back you can find your way home, back to your cave and Ammaji."

She sits halfway between both realms holding the passageway open. We can only see half of her body now, the other half is in our mountain home realm, the cave and where Ammaji lives. We recognize that this is an unusual feat and Anam Cara has learned the ability to bilocate and to be in two different worlds at once.

Suddenly it is clear, this journey will be about the supernatural gifts that come from the inner lotuses and the abundance of that which is given. Anam Cara, working on perfecting the ability of her Crown lotus, is here to help us travel between realms. Ammaji knew she was ready and asked her to attend our journey. She is learning how to use her new gift to help others. In doing so she will be able to keep this ability. And we are learning the gift of traveling between worlds and realms for spiritual growth.

Looking back towards Anam Cara one last time we see she is clearly sitting by a large boulder. Our little footprints are impressed into the earth and have turned to gold. We now know we can find our way back to the entry between realms, by following the golden footprints. Our way is secure and we run off in the direction of the Ocean which calls us.

The River of Spirit

Running over the green fields, with butterflies and bees reveling in our happiness, we feel the air as alive. It is more than just air. We realize we are experiencing that which keeps everything alive, Prana the element of Ether. It is not only air but also the high vibration of light, a substantive presence that is the life energy of the Mother herself keeping everything alive. Our inner knowing tells us,

"This is the presence of manifestation, the energy of aliveness Itself. Aliveness is the emanation of Mother's heart through the universe and cannot be held back. It is constantly being given."

The fearlessness of the monkey sprinting ahead encourages us to scamper off in the direction of the ocean, everything unfolding perfectly as we run, jump and play. Feeling the sunlight on our faces and in our eyes we realize without doing anything we can receive what is just given.

We come upon the white water river that is rushing its way to the ocean as well. The monkey jumps right in. He screams,

"It is spirit water!!" and he starts to drink it. There are little eddies and pools on the edge of the river, all with different qualities to drink. Before going further we decide to sit down with each one.

We drink from the first pool and we feel - *deep peace* -. This peace moves through our body calming any and all small tensions that arise. Our fears melt away.

One of us has moved to the second eddy and calls us forward,

"Come, there's more !" We sit down and taste. As we take a sip, someone says,

"It's - *love and forgiveness.*" - And with that our minds soften, hard edges become like soft sand dunes. We sense our thick ego and emotions dissolving. Images from our past come before us that were painful. Each one resolves as the love touches it and we are left with a feeling of wholeness.

As we sit with the next eddy we sense - *total acceptance* - which takes away all judgment of ourselves or others. At the last pool, all sadness it washed away when we feel - *care of a loving mother* -.

Ammaji's voice is heard,

"This is a gift from the All to your heart. You will retain this knowing as energy in your heart to be used for yourself or others."

Each pool has been a profound treasure for our heart; *deep peace, love and forgiveness, acceptance and care of a loving mother.* And we are given the gift to be this water for others. We lay back in the grass to integrate the overflowing abundance of the All, Mother God, and all that is abundantly given.

The Ocean & Four Elephants

Quite amazingly the monkey, delirious with joy, rises up out of the River on a mighty sailing ship. He has been transformed into its captain and he invites all of us on board. His stature is powerful and determined as he sets sail into the milky white ocean.

Huge rolling waves greet us as we enter the mouth of the ocean. We hold onto whatever we can find to not be thrown overboard, as the power of the tumultuous sea demands our attention. A vision emerges up ahead, but we can't make it out before sliding down a huge wave. The waves must be 50 feet high and this obscures all sight, save for the next ocean wave. As we rise up and crest on the next massive wave, the vision has come closer and then down we slide again. Rising up to the crest of the next wave, the vision becomes suddenly clear and the ocean becomes suddenly still. A giant lotus has risen out of the ocean with a goddess standing tall on it. She is surrounded by four large elephants. They are spraying water all over her. The water wraps around her to become her cape and our inner knowing tells us that her cape contains the gifts, all gifts. And we realize she is the Giver of all that is Given. And we bow to Mother Kamala. She lifts her hands and shines golden light in our direction. The light falls onto our seed pouches.

And as that happens we are all brought awake. We wake up on the grass next to the River where we must have fallen asleep, all having had the same dream! Gathering ourselves up in preparation to return home to Ammaji, we check our pouches. And sure enough inside the pouch all the seeds have been covered in gold.

We sit in awe of the gifts, of all that is constantly being given. The monkey now himself once again, runs off to follow the path of the golden footprints and it's time to go home to our cave and Ammaji.

The Blessing

Nirmala Devi has helped Ammaji into her garden where she is meditating. The little elephant and the monkey are cuddled up together so happy we made it home.

As we gather around to meditate with Ammaji, we notice the air has become very still and a special presence seems to have entered the garden. We sit for hours feeling the new presence that is here. Occasionally we lift open our eyes only slightly and see a peacock pass slowly through the garden. At another time we notice the baby elephant grazing nearby. We lift our eyes again, and we notice the monkey has fallen asleep curled up in someone's lap. There is a great slowing down of time to the point that everything becomes more like a vision rather than a physical experience. Our breath is hardly noticeable and we have the sense we do not want to move as it might disturb the trance-like beauty of the present moment.

With our eyes only slightly open we notice now that Nirmala Devi has brought some bowls with water and bunches of flower petals on woven leaf baskets. Ammaji starts chanting softly and we feel the sounds penetrate our bodies. The sound is transforming the elemental nature of the water and flowers along with our mundane nature. Our physical, mental & emotional bodies are being transformed. We allow the sound to penetrate us deeply.

We realize that Anam Cara is also here sitting at the feet of Ammaji. She is refreshed in a new splendor of being. Ammaji anoints her with the water and flowers. Her new abilities are being blessed.

She can now control her attitudes and hold the door open to different realms. She herself has become a doorway between realms. Ammaji reaches out for Anam Caras hands and holds her palms open and up. And in that same instance a ruby red stone pendant and chain appear in one of Anam Cara's hands. Ammaji lifts it up, blows on it, and in doing so a mantra is inscribed onto it. She places it over Anam Cara's head and the pendant takes its place just above her heart. A light descends onto her and into the pendant and we realize the pendant has also become a doorway between realms.

The Great Door and the Bell of Being

Ammaji turns to us and begins to ask about our journey into the realm of Heaven. We bubble out our happiness and show her how our seeds have all been covered in gold.

"Very good and very important," she comments. "Now as you move through your karmas they will be directed towards their highest purpose."

"I have a surprise for you, " she announces. Ammaji motions to Nirmala Devi that it is time.

"Anam Cara held open the door to the two realms," she says, "and achieved a higher level of awareness. This ability, to hold open the door between realms, starts with meditation," she explains.

Niramla Devi has prepared an exquisite altar nearby with a golden cloth and a flower offering. As we turn to it a brilliant light radiates down from above and reveals a statue of a goddess & a yantra standing on the altar. Ammaji explains,

"These are manifestations from a higher realm. Here, on this level, they are holding the door open to the realm from which they come. As you make offerings to them you are inviting their wisdom to be present. You are inviting their realm to be present. You are inviting the wisdom from that realm to be with you and guide you."

Ammaji puts her hand on her heart and we follow her lead. She begins,

"There is a great door in the center of your heart. It is the door to the Infinite and to the Bell of Being. Enter the doorway and turn around. You will see the door is actually wide open. The door to the Infinite is always wide open. Walk in further and you will find the shrine of the Golden Bell. This bell is your soul. When you enter the door to the Infinite, in meditation, you are entering the chamber of the Bell of your Being."

And with that, the bell begins to ring. It rings peace, love, gentleness and it brings awareness to all that is given. The ringing of the Bell of our Being reverberates throughout the universe. And we feel our meditation as a great doorway, our heart as the doorway to Eternity.

The peacock appears again. He raises his tail feathers straight up high above the ground and slowly shakes out their radiant splendor in a massive arch down to the ground. Shimmering with iridescent colors the feathers vibrate to the sound of the bell. Ammaji adds,

"All of nature responds to the Bell of your Being ringing in eternity." As the words pour out from her heart she says, "And it is simply and constantly given, given to everyone."

We are being bathed in radiant healing light that feels like wholeness. We feel complete as if we were the entire universe itself, all at once, with nothing missing. We feel every part of ourselves being healed by the vibration of the Bell of our Being, ringing throughout eternity.

CHAPTER FIVE

EMPOWERMENTS

The Bonfire of Release

The sound of the monkey shrieking jars us out of sleep. He runs in and out of the cave, up and down the walls. His excitement, meant to alert us, reveals his fear. Someone grabs him to calm him down. The braver of us run to the front of the cave and find the baby white elephant pacing back and forth trying to keep something at bay. We realize a large male lion has approached the cave curious about its contents and defensively hides behind bushes as we come out to investigate.

We calm the elephant and bring her back inside the cave, as we watch the lion menacingly approach. We climb up onto rock outcroppings inside the cave and some of us crouch beside the elephant. Most of us try to find spaces away from the cave floor or go deeper into the cave.

The lion paces the entryway sniffing the ground very slowly, the sound of his breath echoes throughout the cave. After months of blissful existence here in our intimate and protected environment we feel genuine fear. We are amazed how quickly peace vanishes when we feel some type of physical threat.

As the monkey is about to flee the cave to go get help a thunderous lightning storm pierces the sky, even though there are no clouds in sight. From the direction of the cabin a great goddess lumbers towards us. She is seven or eight feet tall with rugged clothing and weapons of all kinds strapped around her body. Every part of her is large. Large head, shoulders, arms, hands, legs, feet. Her hair is ruff, full and long, tied here and there to try and tame it. In our fear we are as much awed by her as curious.

Our hearts pound in hopes that her arrival is a good thing and not a point where our fear destroys our ability to stay present. We are amazed how the mind scatters when it perceives fear. The stronger spirited of us motions to stay calm.

As the goddess approaches the cave the lion takes his place by Her side. And now we realize they have come here together.

She stops at the entrance to the cave glancing powerfully in our direction. In one glance she knows us completely. We suddenly feel extremely small and way out of our league. Maybe we had the wrong idea to even come here? All our doubts leap forward preventing level headedness. Her power is absolute, her presence demanding. She is like a human version of the lion alongside her. We dare not approach and immediately surrender our will. Her gaze agrees with our response and she motions to the lion to follow her. We watch them walk away to the edge of the precipice.

Assisted by the young girls, Ammaji emerges from the cabin. We hurriedly abandon the cave to the security of their presence as they motion,

"Come here with us." The elephant runs alongside. Recognizing our fear they bring us close together as we watch the crescendo of power that ensues on the precipice.

The goddess gathers energy before her, spinning her arms, creating a swirling mass of bramble, brush, and thorny bushes that appear out of nowhere. She throws bundles of it to the ground in front of her. Breathing heavily, over and over she works as she builds a massive pile large enough to create a bonfire. The lion rears up roaring each time she adds to the pile, tearing into the air around him, assisting her in his own way. She has gathered all the stuff of our existence and pulled it out of us. She has extracted lifetimes of debris of one sort or another, none of it matters now. The good, the bad and the ugly are forced out into the open and into the pile.

We now understand why she looked at us the way she did. In one glance she captured the pure and impure from us and knew exactly what to do with it. Lighting a giant torch that she manifests out of thin air, the towering goddess sets the pile ablaze, each flame fighting higher and higher for the sky.

Satisfied with the intensity of the fire, the lion crouches down next to the goddess and offers his back to her. She climbs on and in three huge strides coming straight for us they jump up over the cabin into the sky and are gone.

We fall to our knees and bow our heads to the ground, knowing we have just met Bhairavi, the Warrior goddess. She built the bonfire just for us. As we watch it burn we begin to feel ill and our bodies become nauseated and weak. Putrefying disease exits our bodies and we fall exhausted to the ground.

After disrobing us, the girls escort us to the side of the cabin. Here they cleanse our bodies with the fresh spirit water from the river. The baby elephant assists them by spraying us as well. Murmuring mantras, they wrap us in clean blankets laying calendula blossoms and rose petals inside. Slowly they help us walk back to the cave to rest. The monkey brings us bananas, the girls leave us fresh mint tea and we fall fast asleep.

Fire-nights & the Empowerments

Three days pass as we gather our senses. We are much thinner now in more ways than one and our awareness seems freer or more expanded. The great bonfire has finally gone out and the elephant and the monkey are busy searching through the ashes. Every now and then they find what they are looking for and excitedly bring it to Ammaji.

A fresh breeze begins that takes away the heavy smoke filled air, which are remnants of our mental impurities. Feeling the lightness of our bodies, a mental clarity is evident now. We are experiencing the freedom and renewal that is felt after releasing lifetimes of congested patterns and negativities.

The young girls are sitting in meditation with Ammaji and she stops briefly now and again to give them instructions and guidance. Nirmala Devi wipes away occasional tears as Ammaji comforts her. They have their own unique dynamic together while they attend us.

For the time being we no longer meet Ammaji during the day but rather we are told we will be meeting at night to sit with her for meditation. We rise early to gather flowers and herbs to make her offerings. Working in the garden we tend the altar during the day. We all have learned our chores by now. When we are done the girls prepare us a bowl of their savory rice and vegetables.

We sleep most of the afternoon until Anam Cara comes to collect us.
"We will be meeting each evening for the empowerments," she explains.

We are all certain we need this, whatever it is, after experiencing Bharavi. She takes us to the temple garden behind the house, where the young women have prepared a simple fire pit.

"Meditate and empty out your minds," Anam Cara guides. "You are entering the heart of your journey. There is so much to learn. After each empowerment night you will rest, meditate, and integrate your practice. For one week you will not be expected to do any chores, but rather allow the empowerment to merge with your psyche so you can become stronger."

Fire-night Empowerment One ~ Heart Availability

Sitting around the pit someone lights the fire sending sparks flying into the air. Ammaji slowly emerges from the cabin and makes her way to the head of the fire pit. The smoke billows up and creates forms before us. You can tell she has done this many times before. At times she chants and places more brush and powdered herbs into the fire causing more smoke to rise.

She tells us,

"This is for purification throughout all realms."

The night sky grows blacker as the fire builds. The fire begins to crackle and pop as Ammaji throws butter into it to intensify the heat. The more she chants the deeper we go inside our hearts. Her words are pulling us inward, pulling us inward to our ground of being, centered in the middle of our hearts.

Raising her arms over the fire she invites invisible spirits to be present while she works with us. We begin to feel the presence of souls that have done this with her before. Some are physical, but far away and join in through their meditation. Others have come that are spirits without physical bodies and are attending from a different realm. We can feel all of them now.

Ammaji knows them all and instructs us,

"This is the empowerment of heart availability. Open your hearts to invite everyone that has come to join us." A part of me doesn't want to open up to the others. I feel my resistance and possessiveness wanting this experience and Ammaji all to myself. My heart feels small and I can feel it contract. But then as if she heard me say this out loud she commands,

"Open your heart and use your heart to touch and welcome all beings!"

And as she says this we feel our hearts expanding as if each of us have joined one hundred other hearts. We can actually feel the sweetness of all the hearts that are with us and the brilliant energy of their love. And for me it is unexpected and overwhelming.

"They are thankful because we are making their presence possible," Ammaji explains. Some of us burst into tears.

"Everyone has a different capacity to open," she continues.

"You are learning to be available and to serve any and all beings with an open heart. You have been given this rare opportunity to be physically present in this high light realm where you are totally protected. When you ground yourself in the center of the love, the source of light itself, you cannot be destroyed, eliminated or ended. Yes, the small you disappears but the larger you expands and merges with the life force energy Itself. And your vibration, your availability assists others to learn and grow as well."

And she leads us into the sky of the open heart inside our own heart where there is no limit of love available to everyone and everything.

After the meditation ends, we get up from the fire and walk to the edge of the precipice; still feeling the myriad of souls walking with us. Slowly the other souls begin to lift away spreading across the sky and disappear—but we know we are always connected.

For the next week, we meditate on the sky of the open heart extending love to everyone. Whether we sit in the cave, on the precipice, or in the forest, we have entered a borderless state with our hearts ever more liquid and open. Our hearts have become a deep well of fresh acceptance, available to the All.

Fire-night empowerment two ~ The Golden Key of Truth

After a week of deep rest Anam Cara brings us back to the fire pit.

"Listen to the fire and steady your mind," she invokes.

We sit by the fire with its warm glow, our mind quieting into a steady receptive presence. Ammaji chanting adds more ghee and occasional wood.

After an hour of the mesmerizing combination of fire and chants, she suddenly raises her hands above her head sending a lightning bolt into the blazing fire. It responds in turn by leaping into the air. With a thunderous pulsation the golden key Ammaji wears on her blouse flies into the fire. It is suspended in the middle of it, turning over and over until it becomes red hot. It then bursts out the other side, multiplies, and sears itself onto our hearts.

"This is the golden key of truth," she explains.

"This impression is now on your heart and seared into your soul. Feel Truth through your whole body. This is not any truth but the Ultimate Truth."

We are overwhelmed with this new sensation and we suddenly feel compelled to bring words forward to express this Truth.

"I am whole," someone says.

"I am unfolding," another voice rolls in. And then like a waterfall, a musical cascade of voices ensues.

"I am balanced, I am the Light, I am infinite, I am abundant, I am free, I am one, I am stillness, I am, I am That which Is, I am radiant, I am expanding, I am aliveness itself, I am consciousness, I am the Source, I am home."

The many voices merge and sound as if they are only one voice but distinctly coming from the many. Over and over the Truth is sung into the night. The fire responds, bursting sprays of sparks and flames.

We know not how long we share the Truth but at some point Ammaji begins to leave and we see the golden key resting in its place back on her blouse glistening in the firelight. Our hearts have been initiated into the Ultimate Truth.

With the fire pit still burning we walk to the edge of the precipice. We take in the fresh cool air and find our way back to the cave, our home, our shelter. The monkey and the elephant run alongside. The truth surrounds us all like a blanket and we fall fast asleep.

Fire-night empowerment Three ~ Steadfastness

After a week of integration by resting and meditating, we are brought to our last fire-night empowerment with Ammaji. Tonight only Anam Cara is assisting.

As we gather around Ammaji starts chanting and from the flow of her voice she creates two separate visions opposite her. She directs our attention to them. One is a Great Mountain, stoic and reserved with all kinds of life growing on it and inside of it. The other is a large white Tiger, who begins to pace back and forth. Her posturing indicates she knows what comes next.

"You are going to learn their strength," Ammaji proclaims.

"Their strength is the gift of steadfastness. You need this ability as you lead your life and do your practices. When you walk the path of the MahaVidyas you are experiencing their two main aspects, one is receptive and benevolent in nature, the other fierce and forceful. Both are protective in different ways. One is not better than the other. They are both necessary to bring balance to every experience," she explains.

And with that the Tiger finishes her pacing and lays at the foot of the Great Mountain. Ammaji asks us,

"Stand up. Stand like you are the Mountain. Feel the strength of its steady presence. Now, when you are ready, walk over to the Mountain and step inside of it. As you do so you will become the Mountain. Feel your head as the top of the mountain and your feet as the bottom, standing broad legged with open arms".

We all take turns stepping into and becoming the Mountain. We can feel the strength of its steady presence through our whole body. Ammaji directs,

"Now take this experience to your heart. Allow your heart to be the Great Mountain. This is the presence of the Ultimate Truth. Feel this strength and how grounded you are in it. Nothing can move you from the ultimate truth. Feel it's great gentleness as well.

We can feel the subtle difference of experiencing the body as the mountain and our heart as the mountain. They are two levels somehow. Ammaji responds to our experience again, as if we were speaking out loud and says,

"Yes, this is because the body is temporary. It is strong now but weakens over time. The Great Heart mountain, the mountain of our spirit, grows stronger and stronger. It is accumulated spiritual progress that stays with you from lifetime to lifetime." Then she directs,

"Now step into the Tiger!" And as she says this the Tiger stands on all fours roaring. The Mountain was one thing but the Tiger is quite another.

"Have no fear," she commands. "This is the power of masterful gentleness."

But before we can approach, the Tiger begins slinking slowly towards us, her energy enlarging to twice her physical size. Her eyes meet ours and she locks her gaze. There is no escape.

She commands without words. Put your hand on my chest. And she lifts her head slightly, her eyes never releasing ours.

We feel the immense heat of her life force under her dense fur and it enters our dan tien immediately. At the same moment she sends her massive wisdom power into our eyes, transmitting an amazing strong powerful love that fills us completely. And we realize at the same time we have been absorbed into her body.

"She is giving you the source energy of the universe," Ammaji explains.

"It is the refinement of the Chi Gung Master. A Chi Gung Master will not be defeated or overpowered, but rather they have gathered and refined source energy to use with precision. The mountain is the passive power and the tiger the active."

We feel the tiger's magnificent power throughout our body, her sureness and agility. And then Ammaji directs us again to bring this strength to our heart. Again similar, but very different. Her power demands truth to be present and available at any moment. We can feel the strength in standing for the right and the just. This is not dominance over others but rather an ability to subdue untruth. The tiger leaves each one of us gently laying on the ground facing the night sky while she completes each person in turn.

The nights of empowerment have come to an end and we walk back to the cave. We feel the cave differently now. It is a great sheltering force, a power that in its openness protects us while we grow into the full potential of our soul's purpose.

A steady rain begins to fall. It falls for days and brings with it a refreshing relief from the transformative force of the fires. And we realize the fire called forth the water and they worked hand in hand to create a balance of being just for us. We are integrating the wisdom of the forces, the forces of the benevolent and the fierce.

The Book

After another week of rest and integration Nirmala Devi comes to fetch us.

"I want to show you the waterfall," she exclaims.

Exuding a fresh radiance we are excited to experience our newness and the purity in the air. She has packed the elephant with baskets of supplies to carry with us. We have all shared time with her by now, and we all hold her in a special place in our heart. The monkey jumps up on the elephant happy to have something to control.

"Because of the rain in the last few days, a waterfall has been created," Nirmala Devi explains.

"There we can all share our experiences," her voice was uplifted and joy-filled.

We continue to walk for about two hours alongside a creek that has also reappeared because of the rain following it all the way to the waterfall. As we play our way up the creek the light in the forest starts to pour down over Nirmala Devi and follows her all the way to the waterfall. We realize this is an unusual phenomenon as it is not shining on us but only on her. She has a special energy with her but her little shoes are quite tattered now. I think to myself she must be preparing for new shoes. Maybe the light will bring them to her.

As we reach the waterfall Nirmala Devi unpacks the elephant. Free at last the elephant jumps into the pool together with the monkey. Using her trunk she sprays the water high up into the air so that it rains down over the monkey. The monkey stands still and receives it. Now and then as the water falls over him, the monkey becomes vision-like. He appears as a prince, and when we look again it is just the monkey. But then again it happens, a prince appears, or the captain of the ship.

"Did you see that," someone whispers. We all nod in agreement.

Nirmala Devi unwrapping the supplies is oblivious to the event. At some point she begins to sing. Singing the most amazing song she is like a siren inviting us to her one at a time. She sings and tones music that is particular for each soul.

The monkey then takes our hand leading us into the shower of the waterfall. The waterfall speaks,

"I am the stream of pure light."

And as that is heard it enters our central channel and washes us through and through. This is such a welcome respite to the days of fire practice. The monkey then guides us to sit together by the edge of the pool and meditate on the purified presence that is with us.

"Now you are ready," Nirmala Devi says. She hands us each a simple little book with brown leather covering and leather strapping. "I made these books for you," she happily explains.

"This is the book of knowledge, the Great Wisdom, that can help direct your inner heart wisdom and provide insight" she explains. The light has returned to her shining directly onto her as she speaks. "First hold the book to your heart. Then carefully after reflection, pose a question from your Soul. Open the book randomly and read what you find there."

And each of us, in our own time, hold the book to our heart, whisper to ourselves our deepest question. And when we open it we find the exact words, poems and phrases that answer the question completely. It is like they fill an emptiness, which is what a question is. A question is a blind spot in our mind that cannot yet see the wisdom from spirit.

Each book is completely different. We lay back on the ground and hold the book to our chest. We feel the amazing joining of our friendship and how special we each are.

At some point we begin to look through the book casually to find what is written there. But as we open it all the pages are blank. And we realize this is no ordinary book. It is only written when a true question is asked.

Nirmala Devi shares blessed fruit with us and explains,

"We are each on our own personal journey." She seems to be comforting us. "This book will always guide you to your true wisdom perfectly." We can't comprehend how she made it. But it is not a question you can ask the book to find out. The questions you pose to the book are only questions from your soul posed to the Great Wisdom.

We lay for hours posing questions. The book teaches us that the Great Wisdom bubbles up from our heart, and then is inscribed onto the pages. They are permanently inscribed, both in our heart and in the book. We relish our new gift as Nirmala Devi dances and sings for us.

As we head back to Ammaji we realize the path, the way back, has completely changed. It is not the same as before. It is a bit puzzling so we stay close to the monkey and Nirmala Devi as they seem to know the way.

The Initiation into the Diamond Self

Ammaji has invited us to the precipice for one last evening beside her. We realize this time is very precious and unusual. The evening light is soft and radiant.

"I want to share with you what we found in the bonfire ashes," she announces. Anam Cara brings a bowl of ash and a satchel from the cabin, the elephant and monkey trailing behind.

"The bonfire has brought forth its treasure,"she continues.

And she asks us to join her in meditation. But first she asks us to come close and she spoons into our hands ashes from the fire.

"Eat this. By eating the ashes from the bonfire of release you are completing a full circle of karma. You will gain strength and clarity from having let them go, having offered them into the fire of truth. Offering karmas to the fire of truth releases their samskaric hold on you as well. The lessons learned never need be repeated. Having been transformed you partake in the completion of the transformation by eating them, by acknowledging the lesson."

Then the girls place the satchel in Ammaji's hands and she holds it to her heart.

"This is the gift from the ashes of your past lives," she reveals.

"There were burdens that were neutralized and removed by the heat of the fire, but there were purities brought forth as well."

She opens the satchel and pours its contents into her lap and into the folds of her dress. An amazing pile of cut and polished diamonds of different sizes pile up.

She says,

"These are the purities from lifetimes of rarified karmic progression you have made. These are the gems of your accumulated practice. Just as we let go of that which no longer serves us, we want to feel the treasure of that which we have earned. These treasures sustain us and give us direction. The letting go of the unnecessary clears the way for the gift of our rarified state of being".

She digs her hand into the pile combing her fingers through them saying,

"and these are the gems I will give you."

The ritual begins with us kneeling before her one at a time. The girls attend one on each side. Gazing into her eyes we see they have changed to the color of the ocean and are filled with a light we have never experienced before.

Radiating love and acceptance she whispers,

"Feel the lotuses at each chakra."

And as we do that she takes the smaller diamonds from her lap and reaches inside of us. Her energy expands our awareness and makes our bodies transparent so that she can psychically enter. She places one small diamond above each lotus in the core of our being. Here they remain suspended. At the very last she places one large diamond above our crown chakra. It's tip touches the center of the crown lotus.

She puts her hand above our head and begins to chant. We immediately feel a piercing current of light inside and we sit straight up. The light is a narrow laser beam in the middle of our sushumna from our mulhardara to our crown chakra. It is a current of aliveness of hot energy, the piercing current just like electricity, it is able to move in either direction at once.

As we watch each person go before Ammaji we see a brilliant light coming from high above and she says,

"This is the pure Light of the Source, God's essence, ParaShiva/ParaShakti. This is your diamond nature."

Nirmala Devi begins to cry and Ammaji holds her close. Anam Cara takes Nimala Devi by the hand and walks her back into the cabin.

We continue to watch as Ammaji blesses each person. We watch as she directs a beam of light coming from the highest realm into the large diamond. It then refracts the light through all its facets creating a field of light around our body. The light then travels from the center of the large diamond to the center of the smaller diamonds piercing each one and each lotus below it. As the lotuses turn so too the diamonds. The radiance that surrounds us creates a force field that is at once protective as it is ethereal.

"The lotus is the female aspect and the diamond the male," Ammaji explains.

"Your diamond Self replaces your ego structure," she explains.

"Stand up and walk and feel the radiant splendor of the Diamond Light throughout your body, mind and soul."

One by one we pick ourselves up and walk along the precipice. Each one of us is glowing outwardly, lighting up the dark night like stars. We can hear her words calling to us while we walk.

"Now gather the light into your core concentrating it into each diamond, so that the light cannot be seen on the outside."

We practice condensing the light internally and then letting it out to radiate around us. The pulsating rhythm of compression and release, teaches us how to control the flow of our life energy.

The Precipice of the All as the One

We have been given so many gifts. The gift to be here in this realm of the Great Wisdom is the most amazing gift of all. Standing together on the precipice we witness the beauty of each of the souls with us. The transformation has been and is so overwhelming we cannot speak. The silence speaks for us. And we realize the silence is the holder of the Great Wisdom.

As we look out over to the realms below we wonder if anyone notices we are not on the earth realm anymore. Are we still alive on the earth plane?

And as if called forth, the Great Wisdom speaks,

"Your aliveness exists in every level of consciousness. You can appear or go unnoticed. You do not need your personality to move or alter anything. The purity of your spirit has now become a reflection of the Great Godhead and you help to sustain the All by staying in the experience of your heart."

A great Om is heard reverberating through the universe. And we realize each time it is chanted new souls have merged as one with the Great Godhead. And each time we chant the Om we assist souls to merge with the Great Godhead. Our vibration is so refined that we breathe only light. And we feel the Great Diamond turn above our heads radiating the light all around us and through us.

We are the All in the One. We are the Truth. And these words are heard as Om.

CHAPTER SIX

THE GREAT FALL

The bracelet and surrender

After another week of integration, rest and meditation we emerge from the cave and take in the fresh morning air. Quite unexpectedly the monkey runs into the cave clutching something and as I look closer I realize he has Nirmala Devi's bracelet. I try to take it away from him so I can take it back to her, but he runs farther away.

I walk over to the cabin, my heart still humming OM. I gather some flowers to bring inside and wash my feet as is customary before entering. As I enter I see a most unusual sight. Ammaji and Anam Cara are sitting around Nirmala Devi who is lying perfectly still on the ground, a white cloth covering the lower half of her body and her arms crossed over her heart.

"What? What? She's?" They look up at me and nod, motioning me to sit. Anam Cara, wiping tears from her eyes, is surrendered to the experience. I am in disbelief.

"But she was fine," I argue. "She was just fine. What happened? What happened?" and they comfort me as best they can. And then a tsunami of emotions overwhelm me and I begin to cry uncontrollably.

"I do not understand what happened. Why her? Why now?" I see her little tattered shoes lying on the floor next to her and now I understand why the monkey had her bracelet.

We all take turns during the day to sit with her. My little flowers have wilted and I gently put them on her shoes. Others with more presence of mind wash her body and comb her hair. I cannot bring myself to participate. The pain in my heart breaks it open and I am sure I will die with her. Everyone gathers new flowers and herbs and places them on her body, arranging them with incredible love.

I want time to just stop and stand still but everything keeps moving. The hours keep passing. How is that possible? Everything needs to stop! I suddenly want to hold on to this moment because there is nothing to go forward to in the next moment.

Life has ended as I knew it and I can't imagine living here without Nirmala Devi. Maybe I should go home? I was so cavalier with our time together. When did I talk to her last? What was the last thing I said to her or her to me? The questions never stop. When did she die, what happened? I go outside after some time to get away from it all. But there is nowhere to go. I would run but to where? I would go back in and sit with her, but she is not there. I want to feel her loving arms around me. Now, how can I comfort myself? She is normally the one here for me.

And then I remember, the book! Nirmala Devi all gave us a book! And I realize she must have known, she knew she was dying. She knew, Ammaji knew, Anam Cara knew and so that is why she prepared the gift for us. And my mind swims back to that day and I search through every moment I can remember.. and every moment I can hold on to.

I calm myself enough to go back inside. I notice now her body is lying on a simple stretcher by the fireplace. She looks so different now. Ammaji is anointing her with holy oils and waters and incense is burning everywhere. I arrange her little shoes neatly by her feet. They are so tattered now and I realize she has let go of this period of karma. And she belonged to the villagers that came to Ammaji for physical healing. But she was different as she could see us.

The Great Changing

At the end of the day two men appear from nowhere and they prepare a funeral pyre on the precipice. The men must have been traveling for three days to reach here, I realize.

"They already knew," I reflected. And again Ammaji answers my question as if I was talking out loud. And using her hand in response to me she indicates,

"From my heart to theirs we communicate."

The men come to the cabin for Ammaji and carry her in a sling between them to the precipice so she can perform the ceremony. They go back to carry Nirmala Devi. They carry the simple stretcher, her small body fully covered now with flowers falling off it like tears raining everywhere. Her little shoes are placed on her as well. Everything is happening too fast for me. Logically I understand this is the next step but my heart and mind are having a hard time keeping up.

The monkey still holding her bracelet climbs up onto me, giving it to me. I cry all over again. Ammaji has explained that Nirmala Devi was sent by her family to spend her last months with Ammaji in preparation for her journey into human death. They gave her the bracelet so she could feel them with her. When they said goodbye giving her the bracelet, they knew it would be the last time they saw her. And they knew it was a gift for her spirit to die with Ammaji guiding her soul.

Everyone gathers around as Ammaji begins to chant. This lifts everyone's spirits. Many of us begin to feel the happiness to have known Nirmala Devi and join in with the singing helping to release her to her next journey. We know she can feel us and as the funeral pyre is set ablaze. And we ponder the precious value of time and how to spend it well. The fire burns into the night. For some of us we can move our emotions like the clouds across a blue sky and join into the freedom that Nirmala Devi must be experiencing. Exhausted, I crawl back to the cave to sleep.

The Great Falling

In the morning I wake up and have to realize Nirmala Devi's passing all over again and face the fact it was not a dream. I go back out to be with her presence on the precipice, joining in with others that have already been there for hours. The men are working to collect her ashes.

Cherishing every moment is actually a very hard thing to do I realize. It requires holding, or trying to stop time and this is impossible. My sadness begins again. Some of us go back to the cabin to help Ammaji and I stay with the others on the precipice who are also struggling with Nirmala Devi's passing. We hold each other and share stories. I pull out my seed pouch as we share the story of Kamala. And at that the crow, out of nowhere, swoops down and grabs at the pouch causing some of the seeds to fall off the precipice.

And as the seeds fall I begin to tumble with them over the edge towards the earth realm. The crow swoops down again this time diving underneath me. He turns three times in the air and becomes an amazing white Pegasus. Transformed, he lifts me up onto his back and continues the descent to earth.

I object,

"No, take me back."

but he is not to be directed. He is following the seeds down to earth. And when the realization hits there is no going back I complain again,

"but I did not get to say goodbye."

Looking back to see how far we have traveled, his huge wings prevent me from seeing anything. I imagine the others on the precipice watching my fall and I just want to be with them. Saddened, I dive my face into his mane and give in to the process. He is four times larger than a normal horse and I cannot see where we are going. We fly for hours, maybe days I do not know. At some point I catch a glimpse of a land up ahead and realize this must be our destination. The smell of the ocean becomes distinct, and soon after, we land gracefully on a white sandy beach.

The Great Watching

As he lands I realize there are five others with me each on their own Pegasus. The whole little group, that had gathered in our sadness on the precipice, also fell off. Somehow our lack of inner strength, our inability to adjust gracefully to Nirmala Devi's death, caused us to fall to a lower realm. And we begin our learning again.

We are still too high off the ground riding the Pegasi simply to jump down. Plodding along the sandy beach we see some women and children playing up ahead. And suddenly from the vegetation inland comes a massive group of men throwing rocks and arrows our way in their obvious attempt to get rid of us. We are some sort of invasion for them and totally unwanted.

The Pegasi take off flying and carrying us onto a high cliff way above the beach where the men cannot reach us. They yell for a long time at us but finally give up and we make our way slowly across the jagged terrain and down to another cove that is more protected. Here the Pegasi allows us to get off and we regather to assess our situation.

We all agree that the seeds pulled us down and we realize that these are the seeds of karma as Ammaji had said. And we see the fall from the high Causal realm as a ripening and living out of these seeds of karma. We also know they are covered in gold which indicates we should search for the golden blessing of our practices. This will help guide us through our experience here in the Earth realm.

Some of us begin our meditations and others of us explore over the cliff. For some reason we do need very little food and gathering simple berries is enough.

"We are living off the food of our practice," someone comments.

From the cliff we watch as boats land on the beach. And the same thing happens. A massive group of warriors, better armed this time, drive the "invaders" mostly away. A few invaders "succeed" and take women for themselves. And a grand war ensues. Colonies grow. Villages are made. Populations grow. We watch for months, then years, from the safety of our cliff and the protection of the cove. We have difficulty understanding time now or how long we have been here.

And then without warning a huge rolling wave comes in and swallows the colonized beach and everyone with it. And all goes quiet. Our cove is untouched. Our days are simple as we remind each other of our practices, the Pegasi content to graze on top of the cliffs and never travel far away.

Again and again we climb the cliffs and to our amazement we watch the same pattern on the colony beach. We have now named it Life's Beach. There, the same story takes place, invaders, warriors, wars and colonies spring up, over and over in a never ending cycle, until one day a huge wave comes and swallows the whole story up. Over and over the cycle continues. And we now realize this is the Great Watching. We come to understand the nature of karma, as we watch karmic patterns and the associated suffering play out over and over.

We are permanent residents now and realize hundreds of years have passed. We have not aged but Life's Beach continues to renew itself. We grow very weary of the pattern as it is relentlessly repeating itself. And then after what must be one thousand years of watching and waiting, a massive wave comes again but this time it is so large it swallows us up as well. We are drawn out into the sea and into the great current of time. Tossing and tumbling, we are crushed by the weight of the waves.

And when we are about to surrender our last breath to the ocean of time … we breathe in an ocean of water and our eyes are shocked open.

When we open our eyes we are back in the cave sitting in meditation, as if we never left. Astounded, I look around at everyone meditating and I wonder,

"Did they have the same experience? Was it real? A dream? A vision?" I search for my seed pouch and find half of my seeds are missing.

And the crow was right … I must take very close care of these seeds as they are linked to my awareness, my attitudes, my thoughts and lifetimes of deeds. I walk out of the cave a much wiser soul and I look around. Everything is the same, the cave, the cabin, the elephant and the monkey playing. We are in a realm of learning and time does not touch us the same way as on earth. But it is influencing us. And we know we have so much to learn.

The Meaning of the Seeds

Anam Cara comes to gather us for meditation with Ammaji. Does she know what happened to us? She must, she knows everything. But did it really happen? Or was it only an inner experience? I ponder.

We walk into the garden behind the cabin where an elaborate initiation altar has been prepared. Incense is curling up and dispersing. A bell is heard announcing the arrival of Ammaji. The vibration of the bell speaks,

"The incense is working on the transformation of all perceptions," it says. And then Ammaji appears.

Slowly she takes her place next to the altar and begins to speak.

"There are many levels of understanding," she starts. We do not know if she is speaking out loud or we are receiving it directly in our heart.

"You are now ready to understand the relationship of time to eternity." Ammaji continues,

"Take out your seed pouches." And we all reach to bring them out. "These are the seeds of karma collected throughout lifetimes of experience in different realms. They all have different meanings. The gift of the gold covering allowed you to come back to this realm."

"So she did know! It did happen!" I sit mesmerized taking in this reality. She goes on,

"The seeds have different karmic purposes. The black ones are for a human incarnation, the red ones for active even aggressive life, the yellow ones for illness and poverty, the green ones for helping the beings of the plants and animals, blue ones for helping as spirits, the purple ones are for teaching with an open heart. When they have been covered in gold your karma is lighter and that seed has an ability to transform itself in your life and in others. You can use them to work out karma and samskaras (karmic impressions) in higher realms. You are here in this realm because of one blue seed and purple seed that was already covered in gold.

"That was Nirmala Devi's choice," she continues. She had two seeds left after thousands of lifetimes and she chose to be here with you, to help you. She needed to move into her next incarnation to complete her progress. And by helping you she completed her karma".

And now I realize it all had a higher purpose and I inwardly thank her for helping us refine our energy and awareness, which in turn released and transformed her spirit. I hold my pouch of seeds, empty them in my hand and sense the enormity of their potential to direct my spiritual path. I remember back to when we first were given them and how I greedily grabbed the packet with more seeds (more karma) in it. It seems my very greed was the extra seeds. I feel the impact and weight of my mental choices on my soul's progress.

Someone questions,

"But what if I do not want my seeds anymore? I witnessed the Great Watching and I want to move beyond the cycle of life and death. What can I do?"

"Ahhh….And this is why you are here now", Ammaji responds. "Now you have choices on how to direct your spiritual transformation, your spiritual progress."

Someone else says,

"Can I just leave them here? Offer them to the fire or to the waterfall, or something, anything?" Ammaji responds,

"You cannot just offer them away, it does not work like that. You need to make a choice," she continues.

And on the one hand I am thankful there is a path to freedom from the seeds and the cycle of birth and death and on the other hand, what will this mean, to make a choice?

Ammaji continues,

"As you awaken to this understanding, wisdom and direction come from a deep inner path that rises up from within. This inner knowing gives you direction. It will purpose the seeds, transform them and dissolve them. Only your spiritual progress can effect a change in them. Your spiritual progress is your dedication to your meditation, which keeps you close to your highest vibration, and your desire to help others. This becomes your commitment to refine your vibration."

And we sit as Anam Cara gives us each our own incense. We feel so deeply connected to our life here and the lessons we are learning.

Ammaji continues,

"And then, the next step, is to take the vows of the Sannyasin, which is the path you have chosen as your heart called you here."

And we feel her words in our heart as, YES, this is true. And we realize a deep gratitude to our own spirit that said yes and walked us up the Great Mountain. She calls us to come closer to hear her teachings and to prepare for the initiation of Sannyasin.

The Great Step

"You have come to your choices now," Ammaji continues. "You can stay in the cycle of birth and death, keep your seeds of karma." We look at each other knowingly and agree that no we do not want that.

"Or you can take the Great Step of the Sannyasin!"

"This is the ultimate step of humility and service that releases you from the Great Falling and will dissolve the seeds of karma that bind you to rebirth."

And we know this is our next learning and our next challenge to be awake to the Great Falling and we want to take the Great Step. We are grateful that our lives can have a higher purpose for all and we willingly surrender. We all take out our seed pouches and give them to Ammaji who has prepared a platter to receive them. We pile them altogether and Anam Cara places them on the altar. We remember when we first got them and how we saw them as a huge treasure. But now we understand the weight and significance of their presence and gratefully hand them to her.

"You have all come here for this purpose. You made this choice when you took your first step on the path of the Great Yes. You are now stepping into the path of the Sannyasin, dedicating your actions, dedicating the purpose of your soul and this human existence to the highest good for all. It does not matter if you have taken the life of a householder or a renunciate. You can still take the path of the Sannyasin dedicating your every action to the good of the all." Ammaji forcefully continues,

"And this is the understanding of Ma Kali! She is the Mother of Time and therefore the guardian of Eternity. She is the principal of choice. Only she can help in the transformation of your spirit from unconscious to conscious."

And Ammaji tells us the story of MaKali.

"She controls the spread of the demon by drinking its blood. The demon is our unconscious behavior and unrefined mind. Ma Kali destroys evil forces, which is our addictive grabbing for the material world. She removes and destroys them," she declares.

"Her sole purpose is to wake each of us up to the cycle of rebirth that creates bondage and suffering."

And as she speaks we all huddle even closer together and pull the monkey closer to us. We see Anam Cara adjust the seed platter on the altar. Ammaji sprinkles them with mantras, water, and even throws ash onto them. And we begin to sense the presence of Ma Kali coming closer. And the elephant comes in closer as well wanting our protection. Ammaji explains,

"The chain of skulls around her neck are our myriad incarnations.

Seeing her wear our incarnations around her neck, terrifies the soul and shocks its complacency."

"This was the endless cycle you witnessed of birth, death, and rebirth, the endless collection of karmas repeating themselves. This was the Great Watching. When you ask for Ma Kali's help she brings her swords to cut through the poisoned mind. They are sharp and extremely accurate. You see her as horrifying, but that is because you cannot see her true form yet."

And some of us ponder and are unsure.

"Do we really want her help? Maybe we should take our chances as mere humans."

But Ammaji does not respond to any of our indecision or weaknesses and pushes forward with the initiation. Strongly she declares,

"Through this process you awaken to your true nature and your soul's purpose beyond the mind and the mundane. I, therefore, call forth the power of Ma Kali to release you from bondage and bless you in the Great Step."

And she raises her hands demanding from the sky the vision of Ma Kali.

A whirling cloud and wind turns in the air and out of it a giant appears four times the size of any human. She moves into position directly above us. We see her massive head with dreadlocks flying, eyes bulging, and her tongue hanging long dripping with blood. And as she spins through the air, her necklace of skulls begin clacking. Her clothes are torn and tattered. She thunders to the ground and with huge bare feet. She grabs the ground with them and kneels defiantly with swords raised. MaKali's presence overwhelms our childlike defensiveness and her power alone shakes us to our core.

Ammaji's spirit stands up free of her bent legs. For the first time she is actually standing. And we are amazed as she moves between us and her and then speaks,

"These are the souls of the Sannyasins. They are dedicating their lives to the All," she cries out. Again no words can be heard. It is all related through the actions of the engagement.

"You have been called forth to purify their blood, their minds, and to take their karmic seeds."

Ma Kali glares at us, shouting energetically. No words to be heard,

"Know that I have the power to transform the mind throughout Eternity!" and we prostrate ourselves to the ground. She grabs the seeds off the altar and with one giant lick of her tongue she swallows them completely.

"Yes, they are ready," Ammaji declares. Although we are not sure she is correct.

Backing up from Ammaji, Ma Kali energetically blesses her head while demanding a promise. Ammaji lies down fully prostrated on the ground in front of her.

"Yes, I take full responsibility for them," she commits. And our fate is sealed.

At that Ma Kali rushes back to the sky continuing to turn as a deep purple cloud and a vortex of wind right above us. We can barely hear Ammaji as she continues,

"You are taking the Great Step to offer your incarnation and any incarnation after that to the path of the Sannyasin." Give your body and soul to the earth," she commands.

Our actions and emotions are a mixture of fear and devotion. And we realize this is the reality of commitment when you stand for a truth that will be intended for all time. But inwardly we speak a deep YES.

"You are dedicating your soul and all of your actions to the evolution and spiritual refinement of all beings," and again our spirit responds, YES.

As we lay prostrate on the earth we feel the process begin. With Ma Kali still spinning in the sky above us, we feel our blood draining out of our bodies and sinking deep into the earth. Ammaji responds to our realization,

"Yes, this is considered the Great Outbreath, the letting go of lifetimes of holding."

And as the process continues we feel a huge release from the holding of bits and pieces of eons of reality, which make no sense anymore. They are futile and useless now. And we continue to bleed out. We can't even understand how they were ever collected.

As we continue offering our blood to the process it pours deeper into the earth. We watch and feel it draining down, down, down into the deep recesses of the earth. The impurities are being sifted out, filtered out somehow, someway.

Eventually all of our blood reaches a pure underground river that is the source of all water. The water moves and turns it, washing our life energy clean.

"Rest in this cleanliness," Ammaji continues. And we feel the purity and emptiness of this moment, clean, clear, and refreshed. And after sometime Ammaji commands,

"And now breathe in!"

And as we breathe in we feel how the fresh water and purified blood gets pulled upward into our body, rising out of the earth from the deepest part of the source itself. It re-enters our bodies and becomes our new blood!

"Now feel your blood as the blood of pure spirit! This is the Great Inbreath," she explains.

Ma Kali, satisfied with our commitment, gathers herself up, spreads out into the night sky and we hear a massive whosh that subsides into infinite silence. Ammaji continues,

"The seeds of unconscious karma are now transformed. And they no longer belong to you. No longer are you just carrying the seeds around unconsciously where they can randomly influence your life or lifetimes, no, you have dedicated your heart to the upliftment of all beings. And you will also be given birth in higher realms to complete your progress."

As we sit up, she touches and blesses each one of us with water, flowers, and her endless love.

"Sannyasin," she declares each time. And her spirit returns to her body. She again cannot move her legs out of meditation pose.

Groggy and weak, we lay for hours feeling the emptiness, the cleanliness, the purity in our blood in every part of our body. With the seed pouches gone there is a deep letting go into the freedom of the spirit.

As the night descends, the stars create an arch of protection over us and our human path has become clear. The only spiritual decision or direction to take is that choice, which is made for the All.

The Final Journey

And as we slowly walk back to the cave, our steps are noticeably lighter and a vision catches our eyes on the precipice. A delicate spirit is walking towards us. It is Nirmala Devi and she is walking towards us in radiant splendor. She has been watching the whole time. She walks up to each one of us. As she approaches we can see her more and more clearly. But she does not stop walking, instead she steps inside each one of us, her radiance filling our body. And she says,

"We are now one. Your work is my work. Be the pure Light of Love in action."

And then her spirit lifts up and dances into the night sky. Her inner light, so radiant, she lights up the sky like moonlight. I fall to my knees feeling her innocent pure beauty and cry. She is ready for the final journey into the Light.

She is in the Light and in us at the same time. We feel her as a deep anchor of love in the Light. A part of us lives with her there now. And a part of us has taken the final journey into the Light. We are here, but we are also there. Borders become meaningless. Beginning and ending become meaningless. Life becomes filled with purpose. We have been released from the cycle of birth and death. We form a circle interlocking arms under the vast dark sky of the new moon. We are one, one body, one heart, joined by the blood of pure spirit … We are One.

CHAPTER SEVEN

HEADLESS AWARENESS

Realizations and the Workings of the Universe

Waking early, with the Great Fall still fresh in our psyche we gather on the precipice observing the varied skies and realms stretching out in front of us. Deeply sobered by our experience we feel older somehow. The vision of our last moment with Nirmala Devi swells up from within and I hold my heart. I feel her lifting away, rising up, and merging with the higher realms. I know I will be with her there one day. And yes, she lives in our hearts, but the intersection of pain and love are felt again. The vulnerability of the human heart sheltered by supreme love are experienced at the same time. There is an incredible grace that pours forth and we lay back on the earth to rest again.

Our experience of reality is shifting as we become aware of new sensations moving inside us. We each respond to the freeing of karma differently. Some of us become more surrendered and others of us more energetic.

Sitting together we share our inner experiences, a dancing light sparkling from our eyes. The light indicates our minds are receptive. There is a clarity, a refinement apparent after letting go of the seeds of karma.

Our awareness is learning to access from an inner environment rather than the outer. Our eyes anchored inward in the heart see the deeper significance and meaning of the outer reality.

It is as if the vibration of the universe is revealing itself through our bodies and spontaneously teaching us how to be with everything as it is, in its most refined form. Seeing auras around everything and hearing is natural now. We are hearing music from angelic choirs in the highest realms. Somatically our bodies feel available to collect all spiritual wisdom as if they were a mountain lake receiving the runoff of winter rains.

Absorbed in our sharing, a new monkey appears. He is very furry and has interesting white fur on his face. He seems to be determined to take his place on the precipice amongst us. Our monkey comes out to greet him, excited to have a new friend, and they take off to play in the cave and the trees.

We all agree we need time with Ammaji and head to the temple garden for morning meditation. She can help us sort through the new information that seems to be flooding in from all directions.

Ammaji is already waiting for us. She sees the sparkle in our eyes and our spirits opening to new realizations. As her eyes meet ours, her energy responds with a knowing and without words she conveys; you are all so beautiful in your great letting go.

Then out loud she queries us,

"Tell me about your experiences this morning," even though she can see it written all over our etheric bodies.

We start to explain the pain of the human heart and the grace, plus all the amazing qualities that are coming forth spontaneously.

"Yes," Ammaji explains.

"As you are freed from karma new insights and heart awareness will spontaneously arise. Your heart energy will be able to recover and heal more rapidly from life experiences. Stay close to your vulnerability, feeling the sweetness of the love that is always holding you. You will meditate more deeply, walk more slowly and dance more often!" she continues.

"All your learning will be grounded in the maturity of understanding the purpose of the human experience. All of life's choices are before you," her words wrap like a blanket around us.

"You will become aware of how the universe balances and heals itself in the various elements. Colors, gemstones, vibrations, sound, movement and pranic energy are all available as healing tools. You may learn to make medicines from herbs, plants, or flowers. Then she invites us to look up into the sky,

"You may want to explore the stars to study the movement of the planets and how they influence daily life," she continues.

Lighting incense sticks she begins to chant. She stops now and then to share her experience.

"The universe is revealing the connection between the physical and Source, the Eternal Light. You can now recognize It as distinctive patterns, as It activates Itself, within and throughout everything."

Moving the incense towards our crown chakra and up to the sky, she blesses us; calling the energy of divine wisdom closer.

"You are ready. You are called. You are completing your time here," she whispers. Lifting her voice to the heavens she continues aloud,

"May the wholeness of the Eternal Light bring balance to the universe. Feel this vibration heal you on all levels; physically, mentally, emotionally," she waves the incense in front of our bodies. "May you feel the liberation of your soul" and she sticks the incense in the ground in front of her.

Laying her hands on her heart we feel she has energetically laid her hands on ours as well.

"We can know Source, see the Great Light, working in and through everything. Hone your ability, to keep yourself in balance, to complete your highest purpose. What you learn in this life is carried forward into your next life, as spiritual wisdom is accumulative," she shares.

And with that we see a vision of Devis or Angels carrying baskets filled with gold coins as if to say, these we keep for you throughout eternity."

Inviting us to journey with her Ammaji continues,

"Close your eyes and go into your heart."

And because our hearts are open and receptive she continues to teach us during deep meditation, all without words. Simultaneously we receive wisdom from Source and guidance on the inner planes from Ammaji.

New Journey, New Hearts

Calling out through the morning haze an owl slowly lifts us out of meditation. We renew our happiness and start discussing what we are learning. Absorbed in our, I-can-hardly-wait-to-learn-everything-excitement, we do not notice a small group of men have arrived with pack animals. They are Sherpas that help Ammaji. They have come down from a trek higher up the mountain. Anam Cara walks up to her and whispers something. Ammaji responds,

"Yes, yes, bring her in." Removing the empty baskets from the pack animals Anam Cara indicates to the men where to take rest and food while she motions to someone else to come forward.

A woman appears that has arrived with the Sherpas. Entering the temple garden she goes directly to Ammaji. With hands at her heart she bows to Ammaji's presence, kneeling. With tears streaming down her face she relates her past period of time in the mountains. Ammaji blesses her head with holy water and prayers.

Ammaji turns to us and explains,

"This is Shanti Devi."

We greet each other with Namaste hands. Her gray hair is long and tied down her back in a braid with remnants of blood woven through. She is obviously not from this region. Slightly older than us, she is more mature and we realize it is not in age but in wisdom. She wears the same Kurta dress and pants as Ammaji and is cloaked in a long wool shawl that serves as her coat and blanket for sleeping. We suddenly feel our nakedness in our simple veils. We realize she is one of us, from the earth realm below, but having been with Ammaji longer. She is also on the journey of the Great Yes.

Turning back to Shanti Devi, Ammaji introduces us,

"And these are the new Sannyasins."

We all bow again. Shanti Devi is here to prepare you for the next part of your journey!" Ammaji informs us.

The next part of our journey? Where are we going? I inwardly inquire. And Ammaji responds to us all out loud,

"The next part of your journey will take you high into the mountains where the snow is permanently resting."

"You mean the glacier?" I ask incredulously.

Feeling the concern within the question she replies with a flow of wisdom within her words,

"Yes. It would appear as a glacier to some, but it is The Realm of the Great Balancing. And we need to prepare for the New Hearts."

With that she turns and points to the precipice. For the very first time we see a group of young people gathering there. Arriving from the lower part of the mountain, the Earth realm, they begin to sit in meditation. And now we realize that is why the second monkey appeared. He was leading the New Hearts.

My mind starts whirling as I try to grapple with what this all means. If they are like us they will be coming to the cabin and cave in a few days' time. And again as if I spoke out loud, Ammaji explains,

"Yes, we need to make many preparations for them."

Our vows of Sannyasin have even more meaning now, as we offer all our deeds to the service of others. Sweeping, preparing food, chanting, meditating all become a blessing for someone else. And we sense it does not matter what work we perform. When we set our intention to be of service to the All, we do not create karma. We are staying in touch with the energy of the Divine Heart. Love. Ammaji continues,

"Go and sit with them. Radiate the Mother's love and what you have learned."

Walking to the precipice we join the New Hearts in their silence and stillness. It is apparent they cannot see us.

The sky turning towards the New Hearts greets them in its own way by shining a special light in their eyes. We watch as their eyes turn from dull darkness to bright, open, reflecting the colors of the sunrise.

Smiling, their faces transform. Their congested mental questioning melts away as the Light moves into their hearts. Without realizing it, they are soaking in the wisdom from this realm. Slowly a few more young people start to gather and it seems they know each other in some way. Remembering our own arrival we know they will sit for several days.

We notice they are not wearing shoes and we hear Ammaji's voice,

"Yes, they are here to learn from the realm of the Eternal Sunrise. And just like you they have been called by the Great Yes in their hearts."

Anticipating all the preparations that need to be offered we are happy to be participating in a Great Cycle of ongoing learning and evolving. Looking at each other we realize indeed we are older now, although we have not aged. It seems growing into wisdom is an aging of the psyche and not the body. And we start back to the cave.

Preparations

It is apparent now that we must prepare the cave for the New Hearts. Fastidiously removing our collected belongings, we sweep the cave floor. We are removing any impressions of our personalities or residual energies that we may have left behind.

Standing at the entry we chant mantras and burn incense to invite the New Hearts to a fresh space. And as if on cue a snake slithers up into position by the cave entrance. Taking her place she guards the cave and the transition so nothing other than the New Hearts can enter. We remember her and bow to her work as we leave. Participating in the Great Cycle we are filled with a happiness and fulfillment that no one can explain.

Heading over to the Temple garden we find everyone waiting for us. Ammaji, Anam Cara, Shanti Devi, the baby elephant, our monkey, are all here. Even the peacock has joined. Anam Cara is preparing an elaborate altar that will be used by Ammaji to bless us.

There is also a young girl that has newly arrived from the villages below. Running up to Ammaji she cries out,

"Ma!" and hugs Ammaji.

Holding her close Ammaji comforts her, "Oh, dear, how are you? Come, help the others."

She too will be staying with Ammaji to help and learn, just like Nirmala Devi. But curiously, she is not wearing shoes.

Marveling at the amazing life we have been shown here I suddenly can no longer hold my words back,

"But I am sad, too."

Feeling my heart contract, my true state is exposed, although energetically it is obvious. Hugging each other we all share our feelings of having to leave this life altering environment—the safety of Ammaji and the cave.

Shanti Devi and the young girl begin to bring out supplies for our journey. And because no one introduced her it is not clear if the young girl can see us or not. Shanti Devi responds to our inquisitiveness about her.

"She is just learning. Sometimes she can sense you and may get a glimpse of you like a vision, but she does not fully "see" everything."

She motions to us, "Come help with the supplies we have gathered."

61

And we are now illuminated to the fact that Shanti Devi can control her pranic energy so that she can be seen. She can make her body denser at will. Her eyes acknowledge our observation and she continues,

"We have brought all kinds of nuts, berries, seeds, dried fruits, sweets, honey, and medicinal herbs to make the dense energy rolls, the Andas. These will serve as your meals in the high mountains. Come let me show you."

Crushing and mixing the ingredients, we enjoy a pleasant afternoon. We blend dried herbs from the garden for various teas as well. As we complete another tray of Andas or teas we place them on the altar. Ammaji will bless all the food, energizing them for spiritual nourishment, which will keep her presence close.

Ammaji calls Anam Cara over and they talk amongst themselves. Anam Cara nods and takes a few of us to the side of the cabin to prepare herbs for the ritual bathing of the New Hearts. Others of us go to prepare the porridge, bread, and the seed packets.

And we now realize how all the preparations that had been made for us. They were made by the spirits we could not see and the students before us. There have always been many helpers. We feel honored to now be the ones making the preparations for the New Hearts.

We lovingly pour our heart energy into the food. It flows from our hands, our eyes, and our whispered prayers into everything. We spend hours writing them on the beautiful handmade paper the villagers have made. We complete the love exercise by folding them into little pouches for Ammaji to fill them with the seeds.

Spending our last evening in the cabin by the fire, our work is done for the day. We have never done this before. Ammaji enters and the room expands to fit us all. We are reminded of our first days with her here in the land of the Eternal Sunrise. She reads us a story while we fall fast asleep. We cannot understand the words as she is reading from a spiritual text in Sanskrit. But it does not matter, we lay back in complete trust feeling her words sink into our hearts, as we let go of this part of the journey.

One last blessing ~ Vestment Blessings

Gathering in the temple garden, we awake early for meditaton. Ammaji and the women are tending the altar. Chants are being poured into the offering to make them parshad. As she performs the last blessing for our journey Ammaji reminds us,

"Feel the presence of your heart. Feel the bell of your being."

She blows the incense out in front of us and a vision appears. It is a still lake. We open our eyes only slightly to stay in the expanded presence of our heart while she instructs us.

Feeling our deep heart, a bell rings. Names begin to float up from the stillness of the lake appearing in Sanskrit. "These are your new names," she reveals. And the names flow around us like shawls. "They will give you added protection and focus for your journey," she explains.

We chant our new names out loud. We hear names like Ananda, Satya, Amrit, Chandra, Amala, Amrita, Sat Nam, Radha, on and on. As we chant Ammaji hands us a large bundle to unwrap. "And these too are what you will wear. You will wear your name and these clothes. As you refine the balancing of your energies you will not need as many layers, but for now they will protect you in the beginning of your journey."

And Ammaji reminds us of our arrival. "You arrived in your clothing which reflected your personality and your karmic condition. This revealed your true nakedness, your immature state. Then you were covered with a thin silk veil, the true teachings, to stabilize your awareness and to strengthen and nurture your emerging heart radiance.

"These clothes are the physical version of the empowerments, your chants and prayers," Ammaji explains.

"They were woven for you during these months and therefore are imbued with the strength of all of them. They are a spiritual protection, a shelter, for your journey to the Realm of the Great Balancing. They represent that you have the teachings with you, within you. And you will not need as much outward teaching from me."

As we hold the amazing garments in our hands, marveling at their quality and colors, we see our name woven into them as well. We are given leather and fur moccasins, a kurta dress and pants, and a beautiful long wool shawl.

"Everything you have is now a vibration of your heart, a reflection of your soul. These prayers are also in your food," she continues.

And indeed we feel so much stronger and bigger now. Yet my insecurities reveal themselves and I ask,

"Are we coming back here?"

Ammaji replies,

"No, you will not be returning here, but we are always together."

My heart sinks.

Ammaji continues,

"As you refine your awareness you will see with your heart, hear with your heart, sense with your heart. And I will come to you in your dreams and during meditation. We will share on the inside."

And we all bow at her feet knowing we may never see her physically again. Most of us have tears in our eyes. And she blesses us with her hand on our head murmuring a mantra. And as if called forth from within, our steadfastness pours into our bodies and we feel the strength of the Great Mountain and the Tiger.

Departure & Trust

Having mastered control of her pranic life force, Shanti Devi is put in charge of organizing the journey for us as she can be seen by the Sherpas. Packing the last items, Anam Cara carefully places the copper vessels of nectar and the books from Nirmala Devi inside. Our monkey jumps up onto the piles as well, riding backwards to watch the departure.

Fully dressed in the vestments of our prayers, we turn to look back at Ammaji. Our vestments are heavy but we sense this is from their safety not their weight. There is a deep groundedness of wisdom that has been imparted, which allows us to walk with purpose and inner strength.

Ammaji, with the baby elephant beside her, takes the blessing water from Shanti Devi who has just presented it to her from the altar. With the golden key glistening on her heart she raises her hand, murmurs a prayer, and passes one more blessing through it with energy from her hand. Taking a long grass switch she sprinkles the Sherpas, the supplies, us, and ultimately our journey.

"The Sherpas have the skill and pacing for mountain climbing," she says.

"They understand the gods live in the high mountains and are willing to help you reach them. Between their skill and your inner guidance, they will bring you to the Realm of the Great Balancing," she lovingly concludes.

Shanti Devi silently points and indicates,

"Remember, only one of the Sherpas can see you as the others are not as refined. But they will guide you perfectly and with sincerity."

Turning back one last time, we take a deep bow with Namaste hands to Ammaji, the cave, the cabin, the elephant, to everyone. And we set out on the Great Walk. Even though we are leaving everything behind, our hearts sense we are taking everything with us.

And even though we have made so much progress we realize how human we actually are and our hearts contract. A shower of loving presence floods into us and a heart shaped stone appears in our folded hands direct from Ammaji's heart.

We realize even in this last moment together we are learning how to adjust our emotions. Setting out into the great unknown the inner strength of the Mountain and the Lion come forward. Feelings of courage and bravery melt the sadness and insecurity.

Drawing our pranic energy inward, we set out. We are ready to take responsibility for our journey and hold the depth of our experience like the treasure that it is. We move forward with humility, purpose, and grace in every step.

The Great Walk

This walk is much different than our first. We felt so light in our first walk, we were so tender and naïve. Now we are heavier, more grounded, with the weight of the wisdom practices. Walking slowly, with many pauses as we adjust to the high altitude, the Sherpas stop to adjust the loads. And as always we view the outward experience as a teaching. Adjusting the loads the Sherpas are focused on remaining in balance, reminding us to do the same. We bring our awareness back to our heart whenever the mind drifts to worry or fear.

With every step we realize the deeper teachings are maturing within us. We can hear the Sherpas psychically communicating,

"We have to time our journey perfectly to arrive at the glacier before the winter sets in." And we plod on.

No one keeps track of the days. It is not necessary. Having left the trees a long time ago we become absorbed in the exquisite landscape of the rugged mountains. With each day that passes there is a noticeable difference in our mental composure. Walking in snow, it is noticeably colder. It is very clear that the freezing temperature is calming the activity of the mind. Transformed, even the monkey has the air of a wise old man now.

The Interplay of the Two Revealing the One

Making camp each evening the Sherpas build a fire. Sharing stories amongst themselves they cook their dhal and rice with the monkey running freely between us. Being with the Sherpas we are learning to watch the stars for direction.

Having prepared a warm surface of sheep skins and shawls we lay down on the ground looking up at the star filled sky. A delicate cool air, a presence, surrounds us as we drift into sleep.

We are awakened within our dreams each night to a new vision, a new teaching as the Sherpas are fast asleep. Hearing and seeing with our heart we are being taught the truth of existence.

Standing at the edge of a vast ocean an old woman is seen, moving with the rhythm of the waves. Rotating around her is a continuous flow of day and night. Sunrise to sunset she dances with the waves.

She speaks,

"Everything in life is in a divine dance with the interplay of the two creating the one."

Watching her we see the complementary forces play out. Her breath aligns to the sway of the waves pushing and pulling, as the moon completes a full cycle above her. From her eyes she transmits a teaching; the entire universe, every part of nature, our own bodies, are all in a dance of interdependent forces. They move in an equalized fashion creating a natural balance, homeostasis.

Taking a long stick to the sand she draws an enormous circle with a curved S cutting through its middle, creating a Yin Yang symbol. Raising up her arm she grabs a bolt of lightning from the sky, striking the middle of the circle. Shooting up and out of the ground a massive tree perfectly balanced spins into the air in front of us; its branches reaching full to the sky, its roots in equal form seeking the ground.

Using another bolt of lightning she strikes the middle of the symbol once again. This time a giant egg rises up into the sky.

"Bhraman-anda," she declares.

"This is the condition of all life and the structure of the universe! Everything is the interplay of the equal but opposing forces—positive and negative, male and female. Together they reveal and create the One bringing forth all of life, all of creation," she cries out.

"Music, light, the health of your body and mind, all depend on the interplay of the two coming into balance which brings harmony and health and most importantly enlightenment. Everything in the universe is this harmony, this Light. And together they transfer all knowledge. We are this Light, this harmony."

Shooting a lightning bolt one final time a great human figure rises into the sky out of the circle. Unable to distinguish if it is a man or woman, its body is half blue and half red. She continues,

"Remember you are human and divine. You are not this body but the body of the universe."

Understanding Existence (Sat)

Arising early a voice is heard inwardly from our heart,

"You have entered the Realm of the Great Balancing."

And we smile at each other knowing we are being led perfectly. Loading the pack animals for what feels like our last day of walking, the words from our dream flow forth,

"Remember you are human and divine. You are not this body but the body of the universe."

By midday we finally reach a river and we are so thankful to be able to refresh ourselves. Drinking and washing we see the most amazing moss flowing through the water, caught here and there in the rocks. Reaching for it, it moves away. Suddenly from the river a tall nimble goddess stands up. Rising to full height she must be nine feet tall, thin and completely naked. Her perfection is stunning as her wet hair sticks to her body all the way down to her knees.

She must have been lying in the river to bathe, we puzzle. But our inner sense questions how this is possible. She would freeze to death to be wet and naked in these below zero temperatures.

Pondering this reality, a warm glowing light begins radiating from the goddesses heart and her manipura. Her nakedness reflects the state of inner purity glowing from her open heart. Moving all around her, the energy becomes cloud-like drying her completely, including her hair. Every part of her is perfect down to the grace she uses to step out onto the edge of the river. Alive and in slow motion her hair dances free of her body reflecting the energy of her spirit. Raising her arms she creates visions for us to ponder, one after the other. The visions are the same from our dreams the nights before. Traveling with us, the goddess in front of us now, was the old woman. She can appear in any form as needed and has been expecting us.

Suddenl,y some of the Sherpas scream for they too have seen her. But some of them turn white, are horrified and run. Another stands rigid and mortified. Not understanding their reaction, I go over to him. She is the most beautiful woman ever to be seen, glorious in every way. Moving energetically inside his body, I can see through his eyes. This ability has become normal for us now and important as we can understand someone else's perspective. Moving inside him I become nauseated as his body feels heavy and stagnant, his blood dense and sticky inside.

Looking out of his eyes I am shocked as well. Standing in front of us is the very same goddess, but using a giant sword she has grabbed her own head and cut it off. Holding her head in her right hand she forces it to drink the blood that is squirting out her neck.

At that point two more streams of blood shoot from the open wound of her neck. Exiting her body two smaller versions of herself appear; and equally terrifying, open their mouths to catch the blood. Dropping the Sherpas body I am relieved to be free and he falls to the ground. Now I understand his great fright.

The graceful goddess reappears slowly turning and floating in front of us. Vajra yogini speaks for the first time,

"Drink from the essence of your Heart. This will heal all disturbances in your mind and reverse incorrect perspectives."

Holding his heart, the Sherpa that can see us immediately sits in meditation, murmuring,

"Vajra Yogini, Chinnamasta."

He sees her as we do and directs our attention to the ground underneath her feet, where she is standing on a man and woman in sexual embrace.

"Balancing the human and the divine, her mind and heart; she is in a state of enlightenment. Experiencing oneness, peace ~ Samadhi ~, she is absorbed in the Source of Love." He continues and he prostrates himself in front of her.

"Yes!" Vajra Yogini energetically responds with delight. Transmitting from her eyes she continues,

"When you drink directly from your heart's essence, your physical and spiritual energies will come into balance and you will be at peace."

Appearing behind her an intense light creates a glistening aura, then enters her sushumna at her heart and shoots out the top of her head. She is so bright it is hard to look directly at her. We cover our eyes, unable to see everything. Clearly she has command over her energies and teaches us how she warmed herself.

An amazing dance ensues as her red and blue parts merge back into her body taking their place as her veins, arteries, and nervous system. Psychophysically they become her ida and pingala nadis. We bow to Mother Chinnamasta, Vajra Yogini, whose intention is the ascension of everyone and everything. In her great love she directs our awareness back to our heart.

A thunderous lightning bolt shoots through the sky as Mother Chinnamasta reduces her aura smaller and smaller. Diminishing herself to a pinpoint of light, we stand transfixed as she sends it directly into the center of our hearts. Gasping as her presence enters us we hear her last words,

"Receive your heart's essence. This is the highest spiritual practice."

And we sit to receive her love through our whole body.

Our Passing Days ~ Pondering Existence

Guiding us to little caves, the last remaining Sherpa shows us each to our own. Here we can meditate on remaining steady and balanced in the heart. Walking by his side I sense from within my heart this is our last day together and I look at him. He looks at me in response, smiles and nods his head. Then aloud he says to everyone,

"This is my last day with you."

He walks us to a river with hot flowing water and says, "Ammaji wants you to bathe here. I will leave you here now."

He bows to us, to our journey, and takes his leave.

Sitting in perfect stillness we sit each morning in meditation. We find perfect peace, wholeness, the Source of our being, in our heart. With the nature around us completely frozen, Chinnamasta's teaching floods our bodies with warmth. Everything inside and outside of us comes into balance.

Reveling in the hot and cold rivers each afternoon, we cultivate peace in our bodies and minds. The monkey joyfully joins us and brings us our Andas. In the evening we make our teas on our campfires and sit for hours into the night. Sleeping with the deep presence of serenity in our hearts, silence and beauty fill the nighttime skies.

Each day is spent receiving the warmth from our heart as the cold mountain air calms the activity of our minds. Feeling completely protected, we hear Ammaji encouraging us,

"Yes, yes, this is as it should be. I am with you."

Soaking in the hot springs we lay in the snow naked. Our simple food and bathing ritual keeps us vibrantly healthy. We spontaneously feel and learn ways to move towards peace, to live in peace. Our mind is stable and alert in the present moment, not pulling or being pulled. Our breathing is even, our awareness open, expanded, timeless, is connected to the All.

Dipping one last time in the hot springs, our hair flowing downstream, we rise up and step out onto the snow. Our lungs fill with the fresh air of the flowers of springtime even though none are physically present. Our eyes are luminous and clear, so clear that when we look at each other we can see deep into the Source, our Souls Light. They reveal the brilliant heart within. There is nothing between the heart and the eyes, only a clear open pathway to peace and love. There is nothing between us and the wholeness of the universe.

CHAPTER EIGHT

DANCING THROUGH
THE UNIVERSE

*Long Nights, the Human Form & the fresh
air of pure awareness*

We are so far north that daylight lasts only a few hours. This draws us inside ourselves more and more, staying close to the stillness, light, and warmth of the sushumna. This life force energy around and through our spine is itself a huge warm cave filled with dense prana that becomes the source of heat and energy for our bodies. The beauty here is so stunning we sit mostly in silence as our practices transport us to an inner stillness unequaled by anything we have ever experienced before.

In the active part of the day we walk to the various streams to bathe and become stronger in our pranic energy exercises. We are also guided to practice building inner heat while condensing physical energy inwardly. These practices are intended to help us in transitioning from the human form to the All.

Ammaji's voice can be heard by most of us clearly as we reach deep into our meditation practice of the early mornings. She says,

"It is a great blessing to have a human form. Spiritual progress is accelerated."

We feel the spiraling interplay of the ida, pingala in our bodies as she speaks,

"This realm will free you of the last vestiges or impressions of the mind."

And we recognize our good karma of having a wondrous human form and the reason to take good care of it. We now refer to it as Brother Body, a loving companion assisting us on our spiritual journey to fulfill our destiny. Breathing the fresh mountain air, we feel the purity of our awareness.

Down to our last morsels of Andas, we transition to taking drops of honey from the cave nectar we brought from Ammaji's. Our meals satiate any hunger due to their blessed and energized nature.

It is our meditation sessions, three times a day, that become our sustenance or "meal times." As we set up our sheep skin rugs (that the Sherpas left us) each in our own cozy cave, we sit and prepare to "eat" or absorb our meditation as food. We have learned how to keep a constant fire going by gathering piles of wood for days. Sitting in open-eyed meditation we gaze out over the mountain ranges into the exquisite vastness.

Breathing deeply and receiving the light in our heart is literally our food now. At the end of each session we place one drop of nectar on our tongue, take a tiny fingertip of dirt from the cave floor and place it on our forehead. Energizing walks in the crystal clear air of the glacial mountain tops completes our practices.

Beginning the Inner Climb ~ Pondering Consciousness (Chit)

Deep winter has set in. We experience days of constant snowfall followed by days of intense sunshine. The bright light plays with our eyes and makes the frozen snow look like diamonds. It has been snowing for weeks now, but each of our caves are placed in such a way on hillside rises that the snow rolls away staying clear and not blocking the entrances from the warm sun, the fresh air, or the need to dig out.

When the clouds begin their play of parting we visit the surrounding mountain tops. Each new mountain top gifts a new perspective or spiritual quality that assists our deeper practices.

Intensely absorbed in the heart, we do not find it always possible to walk physically to the next new mountaintop. Therefore we travel to them as spirits inwardly instead. Having discovered sitting together intensifies our learning, we come out of our caves either way to sit and "travel" as heart companions to the next new mountain. Able to feel each other's presence completely while practicing alone in our caves, there is a fresh energizing, enlarging experience in coming together as a group. We observe that sitting side by side in meditation allows us to travel farther or more deeply somehow.

Radiating the clarity of being empty vessels we look so different now. Stepping slowly out of our caves filled only with the Light of eternity, we realize we are living inside the energy of Mother Bagala. Carrying our sheepskin mats and nectar vessels, day by day we feel our mind slowing down and our hearts expanding.

Taking walks farther inside means our meditation periods grow longer. Each mountain top inspires a different dissolving or expanding practice. But mostly it is the exceptional beauty of the stillness that permeates everything that guides our day.

The Opposite also points to the Truth

Guided from inside we are "told" to go for a walk. One of us seems to have a stronger connection to the powerful voice that has called us and we follow her. Hiking out beyond one of the mountaintops we use for our expansion practices we travel farther down, over boulders, rocks, and rivers into a small wooded forest.

An energy shift occurs around us and we feel a disturbance up ahead. At this point we do not question entering it because inwardly Bagala is guiding us. Having been called here for a spiritual lesson, we continue. Approaching the unknown no longer brings up fear or hesitation. Rather, it becomes a curiosity and an opportunity to learn and expand consciousness.

Looking into the distance we see a group of hunters laden with pack animals and supplies. They are ruff and their putrid smell reveals the food they eat. Their camping area is strewn here and there with their belongings, which reflects their attitudes. How did they make it up here without

Sherpas, we ponder. Taking off for their hunt, we are told to follow them. They cannot see us at all, as they are oblivious to refined energy.

Suddenly they come upon a trail of fresh blood that is soaking down into the pure white snow. Apparently a large animal has made a kill, dragging it farther away to eat it. We immediately see this for what it is, the poison and impurities of the lower mind poisoning fresh awareness. Greed, fear, and the grasping nature of the mind filled with desire which makes us "big" in the world is seen for what it is, a stain on the true reality.

Alert with their weapons the hunters follow the trail of blood, when they see what appears to be a bear eating its kill. Since bear meat and skin are valuable they prepare their weapons and aim, when one of the hunters cautions. "No...Stop...Shh."

They realize upon closer inspection it is actually another hunter wearing a bearskin coat. Lowering their weapons a steady snowfall begins blurring their vision, they move closer to investigate. Looking from behind, they see the bearskin hunter busy with his kill. The negative energy is becoming denser and more ominous, but we realize the darkness of it is meant for the hunters, not for us. We continue to follow without fear.

The hunters move closer, interested to greet a comrade of the hunt, when the bear hunter turns and looks at them. Visibly shaken, the hunters turn white as the blood drains from their faces and they become instantly weak. A true monster is facing them, something they have never seen before.

Mortified, their energy shrinks to the size of their true human ego not the grandiose one they pretend to have. Curling back to get away, there is nowhere to escape fast enough. She is huge with bulging eyes, too big for her head and teeth too big for her mouth. Her hair completely matted, hanging down, sticks to the sweat on her face.

She has not killed an animal but has captured another hunter by his tongue ready to cut it off. Instinctively they know they are next. Having interrupted her they are faced with their own mortality.

Appearing horifically grotesque, we recognize Mother Bagala in her teaching form. She has become the demon of their own ignorance which is the opposite of her stunning stillness. Their "loud" nature (the egoic lower mind) has been silenced. She has to appear in a disturbing form for them to see her, which reflects their mental vibration or the condition of their vrittis. Dropping all their possessions, including their ego, they manage to gather themselves together and run.

Running farther and farther away, the scene before us fades as well and only the pure whiteness of silence remains. Taking in the presence of peace a fresh newness returns. Sitting in meditation, beauty and stillness bring our awareness back to the gentleness of the falling snow and we start our climb back up to the mountaintops. Our hearts slowing down, our minds softening, we slowly walk back from whence we were called, to our caves.

Sitting together once again we reflect on the day's lesson. Duty bound Mother Bagala created an experiential barrier to protect purity, the purity of our practices from the invasion of ignorance. Holding it away from us her work is complete.

When we step into the path of the Great Yes, the higher beings offer their support. We are acutely aware that human ignorance, greed or fear can creep up when we least expect it. We take deep breaths of purifying peace to realign our senses and learn vigilance.

The Mountain Tops ~ The Realms of Perfected Stillness & Silence ~ Experiencing God

Coming out of our caves we once again gather to walk to the next new mountain. There arises a calling to beingness in each of us. As we settle onto our skin mats in the piercing cold, the clouds dance their new lesson towards us. Settling our awareness into our heart and to the full length of the sushumna, the diamond top of our crown chakra forms a funnel. Catching the downward spiral of information dissolves our bodies allowing us to travel to specific realities. We become only the meditation experience. The transition was seamless.

Today we travel together throughout the universe as space, pure awareness. As our bodies dissolve they merge with each other. Becoming one beingness we continue to spread out as space throughout everything. Traveling we join a flock of birds in the sky, or float as moss on ponds. We become the presence in a room where someone is dying as we dance into everywhere all at once. Expanding we become the space between everything which connects everything at all times.

We are the vapor coming off the ocean, we are the cloud touching the mountains. People on earth experience us as pure air, life essence, happiness, as we are one body, one purpose, one expression, a formless essence within everything.

We can sense the otherness ~ of being between things and yet being them at the same time ~ space is so pure that we only experience a radiance of unconditional love. This radiance is pure stillness, unadulterated silence, and yet if you were able to touch it, it would sing like a meditation bowl. But we are inside of it and we realize we are having the experience of God, connecting everything, separating nothing, not holding, unable to separate or to judge. These thoughts are too coarse (too rough) to move towards.

Bagala is teaching us to stay in the sushumna while centered in the heart, not to exit even out of curiosity or creativity. We are only the vastness of stillness, the silence of love, the space of radiant light and beauty. And we realize ignorance is separation from God, and innocence is always preserved as it is the stuff of God, Her essence, Her beauty, Her love.

We never know how long we sit until some sort of flower appears in our awareness to call us out. Following her we find ourselves on a mountain top of early spring where every flower of the world is alive. And we know this mountain top is the source for all the flowers on earth.

We learn how the purity of Mother God evolves from Pure Light, to waters, to sound, to color, onto felt sense, smells and eventually she becomes the flower. The growth of greenness on earth and flowers are the first emanation or manifestation of consciousness. And we realize even the flowers have a purpose and a path to the Great Yes. The smell here is overwhelming and its softness carries us into a deep rest.

Ahhhhh….. and the Perspective of the Heart

Hours and days pass. No amount of drama can disturb the silence. No amount of movement can disturb the stillness. No amount of thought can disturb the emptiness. We are full of emptiness and empty in our fullness. There is not one without the other. And there is neither this nor that. The struggle is over. The vrittis are seen for what they are, the activity of the mind which can be painful as they can agitate the body. And we realize this is why there is a quality of youth to those with deep practice, as it preserves their energy.

Breathing in the softness and we breathe out an Ahhhhhhhhhh that can be felt on earth as sunlight, tasted as sweetness, and can be heard as the ocean waves ending at the shore.

Our breath, very deep and slow, gives the appearance we are not breathing at all. Tapping into the source of Prana itself, we are sustained by it and it is our food now. In the sweetest morsel of breath lies the potential for all nourishment as our bodies are being fed through every cell like a leaf rather than eating from the once source of the mouth. Eating in that form is no longer necessary or desired. We eat like flowers now and come out of the cave to bathe in the sunlight to absorb the fresh mountain air. Needing not even our cave, we retreat to the inner cave of the heart where we explore miles upon miles of pristine mountain tops of unending beauty and splendor. Feeling the full length of the sushumna our awareness is centered in our hearts. This is our home now.

Occasionally we place one drop of amrit on our tongues for nourishment or maybe simple enjoyment. It is more than enough as we continue to smell the flowers as nourishment as well. Our eyes have different colors now. This land of Bagala, of perfected stillness is now our body. We no longer feel our physical form.

Every now and then we can feel each other in each other's cave, experiencing each other's energy with no need to formally communicate. Since we are a community, a sister brotherhood we understand each other's inner state. We can share our experience as if we are around a campfire together and sometimes we even do that. Exiting our silence once a week, we share the intimate journey of our Souls, to support each other. No one knows if there will be a change but it does not matter. Every now and then we hear a distant shriek of terror and we know it is Bagala doing her work.

One day while walking to a nearby hilltop we gaze out into the vastness of the mountain tops. The stillness opens a great silence, the vastness pure and empty. Picked up by a swirling wind the soft snow powder slowly falls on us like dust. Collecting on our faces it lays on our lips and eyelashes. As the sun begins to set, a deep magenta light mixes with the clouds and turns the snow pink as well.

The settling snow and magenta light is Bagala's body. She is the vastness before us, the gentleness touching us, the emptiness of silence expanding our awareness. We are in Her and She is in us. Her beauty is our pure heart. And we breathe in the beauty of Her true presence. We feel and hear our heart beating; our heart (beat beat) my heart (beat beat), our heart (beat beat) is Her.

CHAPTER NINE

FOUNTAIN OF GRACE

Senses and Merging as the only option

We rise very early to watch the sunrise. Walking happily in our cozy moccasins we listen to the crisp crunching sound of the frozen ground underneath our feet. Taking in this poignant moment our eyes fill with light, our skin absorbs the warmth, our ears hear the stirring of nature, our senses are enlivened. As the sun rises it pierces our hearts and we revel in the experience of life renewing itself. The sun emphasizing the truth of this moment, unable to use words speaks with light, beauty, and energy.

The goddesses are pointing to the purity that is our True Being found in our heart. Each one found a unique way to turn us toward our True Essence and away from the embodied mind. With the rays of the sun expanding our inner vision, our Spiritual Heart is seen. It shines as pure beauty, a constant ongoing reality, God with the flavor of peace, love, acceptance, wisdom, beauty. We are free in the body and beyond the body, like a flavor that is being felt in This moment. And IT is the All in all moments.

We gather to ponder our first day in the cave where the rainbow light appeared and moved through us.

"Remember," someone says, "remember the rainbow light?"

"Yes," someone else replies, "it was the Mothers appearing in various lights. They colored us with their wisdom."

Someone reaches for the incense to bless our day. Watching the dancing smoke reveals a teaching.

"Look," someone says, pointing to the smoke of the incense.

"It reminds us that the formless is always with us, around us, caressing us, healing us."

We all nod at the same moment, understanding that the Divine Mother is with us even in the simple burning of incense. The ultimate truth is found in the most ordinary of moments.

"Look, She is dancing her formlessness, the formlessness found in this moment."

"Yes, it is her love," another replies. And we realize the mind often denies such simple events. Yet her love is speaking to us and reminding us our very senses are meant to know union with Her.

We take Her in by breathing her healing essence of nature. Our nervous system relaxes, calms, and opens. Our heart is teaching us that the beauty of smell is one way the formless can speak Its subtle language.

Catching our attention, one of our first senses to develop, is that of smell. Therefore the sense of smell is the closest to reunion. We are very close to reunion with God when we are aware of the sense of smell. We eagerly enjoy the fresh morning air, fresh God.

Studying any beauty we find It, Her, the True Reality, the formlessness that speaks or gives form to everything. A scientist studying the miracle found in cell biology, an electrical engineer studying how light is created, the geneticist studying gene patterns, all forms lead to the formless and the formless informs all Forms and patterns. Even disunity of thought, discordant sounds "requires" or "requests" unity or harmony be resolved, to be restored, or healed, calling it to completion. All ordinary things lead to the ultimate Truth, the All, to God.

And a vision appears in front of us. It is an exquisitely beautifully woven shawl, floating in the air, made of the fibers of heaven. It is speaking to us of form and formlessness interwoven. The interplay of duality is seen as creation bursting forth. And in the wisest of moments we realize the most ordinary truth, creation is a boundless interplay of love and stillness.

The Ultimate Transformation (Ananda), Heart Explosion & the Constant Falling of Grace

And in an extreme moment of union with the morning light, with our minds steady and still, our heart expanded, we become released or transformed into what can only be called Bliss, Ananda. Inside our body a perfect vibration is experienced. The mind has been driven so deep into the love that it can only expand, or merge with the love. There occurs a bursting inward, an explosion in our heart, so intense it calls forth a massive waterfall to appear physically in front of us. Our inner explosion into love has become a physical reality.

The sound is deep and overpowering. Its crescendo increases and lessens as the water pours down from above, falling from where we do not know. Is it coming from a higher region above us? Or is it the waterfall itself that is the higher region? We do not know, but what we do know is this is not an ordinary waterfall and we are called to interact with it, play with it. We move in and out of it. Sometimes we walk back farther out, to try and see the whole of it. But we cannot see the top. We are struck with how magnetic the joy is, the love is.

Our awareness is fully captivated. And we are compelled to jump back into it. Pulling us into Itself, we can barely see each other with the sound and movement of the waterfall being the total experience. The rushing water is so loud that no voice could be heard. Only our eyes can "shout" the overwhelming joy, bliss, love we feel, and share with one another.

A wisdom being makes Itself known. The waterfall is an energy phenomenon we are inside of, it is Mother Sundari. The joy, love and bliss that She is, is pure grace. We call out her name with our hearts as our voices cannot be heard,

"Glory to the Queen of eternally descending Grace!"

Looking back we realize this "water" was present in the beginning of our journey as well. It was the soma nectar dripping from the walls in Ammaji's cave. We remember how we carried it with us in our vessels to the mountaintops. But now it has manifested in its fullest as Ananda, Mother Sundari, the waterfall of loving Grace. This is the Source. She is so captivating we do not want to leave her and actually we are not sure we can. Light flies out of our hands and colors stretch out from every cell in our bodies. At some point we gather together to stand alongside of Her, to witness her beauty. But the magnetic nature of her love pulls us back inside the waterfall where we are absorbed again. We dance in her, play in her. Visions of our journey come flooding forward like a life review: our first walk, the cave, Ammaji, Anam Cara, Nirmala Devi, the baby elephant, all the different Mothers, the meditations, the lessons, and on and on. The love and bliss are re-felt, re-experienced but expanded a million times. Coursing through our bodies, minds and hearts, through every living cell, all we can do is smile at each other with extreme tenderness.

Magnetism of Grace and Her Offering

And finally we let go of trying to see the full length of the waterfall, Her Grace, or each other. In so doing Her magnetism pulls us into her heart completely and we realize we will never be this form again.

Inside the waterfall we let go with the intention to fall but there is nowhere to fall to. We just continue to let go which feels like falling but without fear. And falling becomes flying and viewing or seeing, which is a knowing, along with the overwhelming infusion of the experience of love, joy, bliss that is Her GRACE.

Our mind is conditioned to falling from this height as ending in death, but this falling is a falling with complete trust. We feel this deep trust, this deep letting go as melting any holding in our mind. All previous self surviving conditioning lets go. But at the same time we do know we are dying to our old form.

But if this is death then we welcome it. We have no fear as only joy greets us, loves us, carries us. The water goes over us, through us, and sometimes we feel ourselves as spirit bodies but sometimes we are simply the falling water itself.

If this is the experience of death then we need no fear. Our fear-filled words around dying are absurd and could not be farther from the actual reality. We are becoming more and more alive! And so we rename death: Jumping into Joy and Unending Bliss, Ananda!

We begin one last fall and we see each other turn into rainbow light. We smile, dance, and touch the essence of Mother Sundari. We breathe in Her essence as we spread out and remember the Realm of Perfected stillness in the glacier mountain tops that held us last. Some of us disappear altogether and we sense they will never leave the Light. The rest of us continue to fall down down down, turning like leaves.

Suddenly we see the earth below and a vision of a mystical River appears. Absorbed in our sensation of falling we sense an exquisite soft landing as if we were now snow. A mystical mist from the River envelopes us and the scent of the flowers of spring return to us. The essence of grace is covering us, as Mother Sundari offers us to the Mother River.

The Bowl of the Heart and the True Yogic Position

Looking around, we notice we have bodies once again and are sitting in meditation. Our awareness delicately drifts back into our human forms. Sundari's nectar is tasted upon our tongue and we swallow Her into every cell. Her magnetic essence is pulled into a pearl of sweetness deep inside our heart where She resides forever. Whenever we need to, we partake in her sweetness, her gentleness, we remember the waterfall of her unending Grace in the middle of our own heart. We know this source can never leave us.

As the mist parts our vision clears and we begin to recognize each other. Sitting in Perfected Stillness, our hearts have become giant bowls of stillness, a love that never ends. Pooling up, the mist has settled down into the bowls as deepening water. The water reflects our inner state. Our mind, surrendered, resting, being carried is liquid in the vast container of the heart. We hear Ammaji's voice,

"This is the True yogic Position." We remain completely still here.

As our vision clears the flow of the River comes into our awareness in front of us. A swelling of inner joy pours forth and we know not how long we sit, but we know we must.

We take one last look at each other, close our eyes and enter our hearts. All is love, All is bliss, All is peace, our hearts are whole and complete, nothing is missing, All is given and All is never-ending...She is the All, and the All is GOD.... GOD is Ahhhhhhhh.....llllllll.

83

CHAPTER TEN

SURRENDER

Understanding the Flow of Life

With the River flowing in front of us, as we sit at Her edge in the morning mist, our meditation guides us to be aware of *the flow* inside of us and around us. We become aware of the flow of the blood in our body, the flow of our breath in and out, the flow of consciousness through our psyche, the flow of the ida and the pingala nadis. We become aware of the flow of love from our heart into the world and coming back to us like a giant infinity circle and the flow from God to us and back to Herself. Everything is in its natural flow.

Our inner vision clears and we see on the inner plains that the glacier from the highest mountain, where we learned the Light knowledge from the Great Mothers, is the source for the River Ganges here in front of us now. As the glacier melts she flows wisdom and grace, and this is the very water that forms the many holy rivers in India. We now understand how the subtle becomes manifest and how all the spiritual information, and the inherent spiritual potential is just naturally flowing within the physical river itself.

We sit to listen, to hear Mother Rivers' voice, to experience Her teaching. Her flow is her outpouring love and her words. Sitting with Her, the realm of perfected silence is continuously felt. Here by the edge of the river knowledge is manifest by the Mother Matangi flowing like a river.

A larger cycle is explored when we see that the river mist becomes clouds, the clouds create rain, and rain returns to earth and the River. This flow becomes a blessing for everyone and everything, as it is wisdom which is raining. Wisdom permeates everything. There is no part of our universe that is separated from or without the highest wisdom. After months of journeying it is our refined senses that allow us to realize this. Sharing the presence of wisdom, stillness and peace is our true function, true purpose, our joy in this life.

The human heart has healed in such a way that it knows it is completely seen and loved, it is safe and it is home. The soul wants for nothing as we gaze at the flow of the Mother Ganges.

The river flows as pure God and also represents the flow of life. Our heart tells us the very flow of our life IS God. Everything happens on the river and it is all a part of God's plan. Every part of our life, life's experiences themselves are blessed. It IS the journey that is holy.

The mist thinning begins to lift and we see more people around us. Carrying offerings, little woven leaf boats with flowers and a candle inside, the devotees place the offerings in the water. The Mother River receives the offerings as prayers.

Some of us join in. Pulling our leaf boats close to our hearts we fill them with kindness and all the wisdom we've been shown. We murmur,

"May these prayers go into everyone and everything."

Some of us are gleeful, others of us begin to cry.

As the mist clears we make our way to a large viewing platform near the river's edge. To each side of us are long rows of stairs stretching 100 yards wide and more than 50 steps deep, some covered by the river itself. In the ebb and flow of the rains more or less of the stairs can be used.

On the other side of the river is a vast flood plain. As the sun rises on the horizon it is mirrored by an inner Sun rising in our hearts. As the physical sun slowly emerges, the sun in our heart moves up through our chakras one by one. When the physical sun frees itself from the horizon, our inner sun has landed at our crown chakra.

Sitting in meditation with our eyes barely open, everything is moving in slow motion. As our earthly reality becomes more grounded, our vision enlarges. Around us are thousands of people lined up to bathe in the river for the liberation of their souls. Mother Matangi receives them all.

A little distance away hundreds of small dolphins appear playing on the water's surface. Their movement was a communication to listen to their teaching. As they crest and dive, they teach that knowledge is always available just under the surface of daily activities. Playing while they swim conveys,

"As you swim through life, keep your hearts light. Wisdom will come easily, as needed, when you stay close to your playfulness. Allow your childlike nature to come forward. The All is stored in your heart. Knowledge will open naturally as you listen within."

We surrender to flowing and allowing as a new way of learning.

The Integration & Initiation

There is a commotion behind us and the sea of people around us begins to turn to an event that is approaching. Everyone is pointing,

"Look, look!"

As our eyes scour over the crowds to understand what they are energized about we notice how the people begin to move and part. They are making way for a procession of some sort. And slowly but surely an amazing vision appears.

Durga riding her lion is slowly moving through the mass of humanity. She has come down from the high mountains to bathe in the River and perform a ritual. She is regal and seen in her full glory. Covered with all types of amulets and weapons, her hair is flowing long and full down her back. This signifies her Powers are complete.

She is heading straight towards us. Everyone lowers to the ground as she passes. Surrounded by various animals, attendants, and a white Bengal tiger she is followed by our monkey! Lumbering slowly behind him is a full grown white elephant. Our inner knowing conveys this is the baby elephant but in her mature form. And we suddenly realize that she was always mature but appeared to us as a baby in order to interact with us.

Our senses are overwhelmed with the sights, smells, and fullness of the love and life essence that is present. There continues to be no need for words as they would only diminish the quality of the wholeness we are experiencing.

Durga has bundles of flower garlands draped around her neck including piles in baskets that are strapped over the animals. The flowers, brought with her from the highest realms, are bursting with their full potential of life giving healing powers.

The monkey runs ahead to the River, gleefully plunging into the wisdom light that it represents. Durga slowly dismounts from the lion, her attendants lifting the baskets of flower garlands.

Focused on the monkey, he returns from the river to surrender at Her feet. Reaching out to bless him with holy water he rises up and transforms in front of our eyes. As he stands to his full height we recognize him as Hanuman, the Monkey god, God's most humble servant.

Durga places garland after garland around his neck blessing him for his work to accompany souls on their highest journey to truth. Dropping to the ground in profound gratitude, we realize he had been with us all along.

Durga purposefully turns, directing her power into us with her eyes. Without words she pulls our attention. Her eyes become the source of love itself, God throughout the universe within everything, is radiating from Her eyes. Her head enlarges and her crown chakra opens wide as we focus intensely on her gaze. Everyone moves back as her energy expands. A great space is created around her and yet we are intimately engaged in the love her eyes are generating.

From Her place on the River she calls all ten MahaVidyas, all mother goddesses to come forth. And as she does this the attendants approach us with the baskets of flower garlands they have brought. From nowhere and everywhere the mothers appear. They walk with the animals that attend them. The parts of nature that represent them appear inside their auras. And we see the whole journey we experienced brought before us.

And then Durga motions to each one of them and one at a time they float towards her. The crowd's voices rise up with the event and sing mantras and cry out as they watch the goddesses rise above the expanding crown of Durga's head. One by one they slowly spin and descend into her. And each time another Mother descends into Durga her attendants place a flower garland around our neck and another and another, one Mother at a time.

For a brief moment on Durga's face you can see the goddess' face as they enter her; Dhumavati, Bhuvaneshwari, Tara or Kamala, each one, Bhairavi, Kali, Chinnamasta, Bagala, Sundari, Matangi, one by one. And then Durga's face reappears. We feel the deep presence of each Mother blessing us as the flowers are draped around our neck, one garland after another, one Goddess blessing after another. Her divine smell fills our lungs and goes deep into our being. We feel ourselves merging with the scents and we become as light and delicate as the scent of a flower.

The Mothers are returning to travel as one, as the Divine Mother Herself. And then our vision is drawn further back inside Durga's core energy and there we see Ammaji. Our hearts burst in knowing her simple life appearing on the mountain top for us was created for our benefit. We could never have understood *this* vision that is occurring in front of us now, in our immature state. So she diminished herself to a form we could relate to. Everyone around is watching. As we feel the weight of the garlands around our neck we feel the weight of our humility.

Her initiation is complete, she has taught us how to conquer the mind, how to mend our hearts, how to love endlessly, how to be strong in the face of adversity. She has given all her love, all her wisdom, and installed more for our future growth. We hear some words drift through the air or our minds, we know not which, "You will be the bearers of happiness and health for many in this life, guiding them to the Truth and their true selves. You are all healers now." We use the flowers around our neck to soak up the tears of joy that stream down our face as we receive her words.

And then as Her crown closes she walks slowly back to the lion who crouches down low to lift her onto his back once again. The mass of humanity starts to part as they walk back toward the mountains. And then they lift into the sky and disappear.

On the ground only piles of flower petals and stardust remain. We collect some in our pouches and lie on the earth by the river. The hordes of people slowly disperse. We sit up and look at each other one last time. We can see our journeys now and into the future. By looking deeply at each other we are blessing each other's path.

We see how some will stay here by the side of the river in complete nakedness and will spread ash on their bodies. Others will dress in fine white cloth and chant mantras. Others will sit by a fire stirring the eternal pot of truth to share it with whoever comes to listen. Still others will serve as teachers or corporate executives. But all will be an example of truth and beauty wherever they are. We all have our place. We will always be connected through the play of time and eternity and on the path of the Great Yes.

The North Star of the Heart & Surrender

And as the night descends upon us the stars once again claim their place in the sky to guide us home. The Sherpas taught us how to follow the North Star and we remember every part of the journey. We hear Ammaji's voice calling us to lie on the earth and surrender to the love, surrender to the truth, surrender to the night sky, surrender to the flow of life and the Mother River. Surrender is the highest truth because it is in surrendering that we become the love and the light.

Lying in deep surrender we feel our bodies expand to become an endless ocean. A deep trust is felt as we let go into the earth which is carrying us as a vast deep formless ocean held by the Earth's embrace. All the stars are reflected in our ocean body.

In our liquid state with the reflection of the heavens inside of us, our eyes scan the stars and our awareness scans our heart. Finding the North star in the sky we find it duplicated in our chest as our heart star, in the deepest center of our being.

We have inner verification that our mountain journey was our Heart's journey on the path of the Great Yes. It is always with us. We are always guided when we lie in the ocean depths of our heart. All is given, all is known, and all is never ending.

THE PATH OF THE MAHAVIDYAS,
the Great Wisdom Mothers

Each of the Wisdom Goddesses is an aspect of Durga. Durga guides us back to our heart, our Spiritual Heart, as our essential self, our soul by showing us her ten inner forms. Meditation in the heart is her gift to us. She leads us through our human self to the Divine. She is a path to enlightenment.

She guides us, walks with us through the human story, giving us strength, courage, humility, honesty, and resolve to travel this life with dignity and compassion.

The following descriptions are meant to be a starting point for personal study. To understand the movement meditation associated with each Mother Goddess, please see Ruth Davis' book, Sacred Movement Ritual, Yoga Philosophy in Movement.
www.TheMotherPractice.yoga

And where Ruth teaches:
www.SilentStay.com
www.AssisiRetreats.org

Durga

Durga is the Guru and holds all ten Mother Goddesses inside of her. As we practice devotion to Her we become one with Her heart. And we recognize She is our Spiritual Heart. There is no separation.

Therefore all aspects living in Her are living in us. Through the story and contemplation, these aspects come alive in us and we become aware of these aspects influencing our lives.

Each aspect points us back to That which is an ongoing reality, the love and peace that is in our heart, that IS our heart, our home, our being, all that is.

The Mythological Story of how Durga came to be

"The ten wisdom goddesses are originally associated with the myth of restoring the Vedic teachings. According to a story in the Shiva Purana (verse 50), a demon named Durgama took control of the four Vedas by a boon of the Creator, Lord Brahmananda, and through them gained power over the entire universe.

This caused a tremendous drought on earth for many years in which all creatures suffered greatly. Hence the Gods called upon the Goddess to save the world. The Goddess, who always responds to the wishes of Her devotees, first eliminated the drought and filled all the waters of the earth.

Then the Gods asked an additional boon to destroy the great demon and reclaim the Vedas. In her battle with the demon, the Goddess brought ten great forms out of Her body—the Dasha Mahavidya—and then took the forms of innumerable Goddesses.

As the conqueror of Durgama, the Goddess was named Durga. The Goddess is the Divine Word and the Vedas, who periodically renovates the teaching in order to sustain it in this world bound by time and death." David Frawley

Dhumavati

Known as:

The Womb (Void) that is empty, the Virgin, the Wise Old Woman, the Great Pause

Experienced as:

Silence, stillness throughout everything, emptiness, fog, darkness, night sky, new moon, pure potential, ocean of being, merging.

Governs:

Transitions of all kinds including birth and death. Hiding the movement of God traveling into the body and back to him/herself. Here we forget our past life(s). She is the Great Pause. Emptiness reveals pure potential. It creates clarity, availability, openness, non-holding, nakedness, vulnerability, purity. Silence is the fundamental principle that connects everything. It is likened to the string that connects all the beads on a prayer necklace. The string runs through everything holding all the beads (life activities) all in peace.

Heart Meditation of Dhumavati:

Slowing down, we come inside. So much of our time is spent collecting the impressions of the outer world. These impressions sink inside, we get filled up with the confusions in the world, the news, life pulling us this way and that.

In meditation we empty out, we let go of all the impressions, the activities and are welcomed to an inner space that is open, empty, and free. Let go and come inside. Breathing, softening we empty out. We let go and breathe into our hearts. Our hearts are the space of the Infinite and as we empty out we can feel the space of the infinite more. This space opens, grows wider and wider. It expands into a vastness without borders.

This is our empty openness, the Great Pause, silence. Here we dive into our ocean of being. We receive the vastness here, the silence. We spread out, in the emptiness, the space of pure being. We soften our minds to enter the space of the heart, Presence, the Great Pause. Here inside the vastness is the bud of pure potential. Mother Dhumavati is the vast pure space of being, empty and open.

Movement Meditation:

Standing in stillness, open, aware, alive, empty, present

Bhuvaneshwari or Mother Mary

Known as:

The Womb (Void) that is full, the Pregnant Mother

Experienced as:

Awakening, Samadi in the heart, enlightenment, absorption in the presence of God in our heart, wholeness, awe, acceptance, unconditional love, pure awareness (the Source/God) is in our heart (Spiritual Heart) which is our essential Self; true self, true nature, pure awareness, playfulness.

Governs:

Enlightenment, giving birth to the Light in our heart. She is the **fullness of the All** giving us a human form for the Light of God to embody. She reveals the Light in us. She holds us in complete love at all times. She is our ground of being. We can feel our childlike awareness, our innocence.

Heart Meditation of Bhuvaneshwari:

We rest our awareness in the center of our hearts. We let go of our wants and desires. We let go of wanting more, achieving more. Inside our hearts completely surrounded by the love of the Divine Mother we have enough. Going deeper and deeper into our hearts we come to the Light of our being. We stand in this Light, this Light is in us. We spread out in the Light, we receive it, we are it. This Light is God in us, the Christ Light, the Buddha nature, our soul. Feel the safety here, the wholeness here. Here we are enough, we are whole and complete. Standing in the Light we radiate in all directions like a beacon of Light, beaming our soul, our love, to everyone and everything.

Movement Meditation:

We step forward, symbolizing stepping to the center of our heart, our ground of being where we are completely seen and loved, we are safe and we are Home.

Tara

Known as: The Mother of compassion and Primordial Sound OM, the Word, Logos

Experienced as:

All creativity, music, sound, empathy, understanding, forgiveness, self acceptance, protection, thankfulness, milk & honey of compassion, wonder.

Governs:

Deep seeing, gratitude and compassion, our natural talents, clarity of purpose. True sight means that I am the other and the other is me, I am God and God is me, fully understanding reality. The dynamic of human and divine is revealed.

Heart Meditation of Tara:

Go downward and inward into your heart. Rest deeper and deeper inside. We let go of separateness, we let go of judgements of ourselves or others. These judgments block our view of life, harden the heart and stop us from engaging the mystery of life. When we let go of judgements we engage our hearts.

Let go of thoughts, breathe into your heart, feel the love here, feel held here, feel the safety here. Allow this love to wrap around you, feeling the acceptance here. This is the arms of our heart carrying us, protecting us. We are completely seen. In every corner the light of love comes. We surrender. We are accepted for who we are as we are and we let go even more. We lay in unconditional love spreading out inside. Every part of us is held, we cannot be rejected.

We are loved completely, we are loved as we are. We bow our heads in gratitude to this Great Love and absorb Its presence.

Movement Meditation:

I am thankful for my practice. I am thankful I remembered my practice and that I am able to do it. Hands come to prayer pose.

Kamala or Lakshmi

Known as:

Mother of beauty and abundance

Experienced as:

Abundance of everything beautiful that is present everywhere at all times; wealth, overflowing, perpetual opening of anything i.e. flowers, plants, mind or heart, opportunities, radiant love of the heart, siddhis.

Governs:

The knowledge that all love, beauty and abundance are constantly being given. This points us to the true abundance and richness (wisdom) of our soul that is inside of us. All beauty that we see outside is a reflection of the beauty of our Spiritual Heart unfolding continuously in the center of our being.

Heart Meditation of Lakshmi:

We soften inside. We let go. We lie back into our heart, into the calm. We let go of feelings of lack, "I need more of this, I can't live without that." Here in the heart inside our heart nothing is missing. Everything is given. So often we search outside to be completed. "Oh, if only I had a better job, more money, a better relationship, better health."

Slowly we let go into the center of our heart. Here the lotus flower of our heart comes forward. This giving flower holds all gifts, all love, all wisdom. As we feel deeper and deeper into the flower of our heart we come upon a well, a well filled with peace, kindness, life energy. It pools up from within. We lay in the well of our being. The gifts from this well are constantly being given. We receive them through our whole being. These gifts are our true treasure, they are the diamond light of the soul, its wisdom, its beauty, its peace. Rare jewels of every kind are in us, revealed to us. Our inner treasure is our golden beingness and our endless giving nature.

Movement Meditation: I feel all the beauty that is around me. I bring it into my heart and it flows through my whole body. Reaching up we gather all the beauty and bring it into the heart.

Bhairavi

Known as:

The Fire of Truth, I am That

Experienced as:

Kundalini (Shakti) energy, upward moving joy, aliveness itself, fire, intensity, diamond mind, rarified states of consciousness, honesty, heart fire.

Governs:

The refined (revealed) brilliance of the soul, I AM. She takes away the dross/dirt of the human incarnation to reveal Its true essence (God). She is the fire of truth that removes everything that is not needed (untrue, of the mundane world), out of the way. Reveals the ultimate truth like a treasure of diamonds (gifts of spirit; wisdom, all loving attributes, all pure intentions, all spiritual realizations) that already belong to us. Her fire makes diamonds out of the coals of karma. All parts of our human self are purified to reveal the rarified soul.

Heart Meditation of Bharavi:

Letting go we soften inside. We feel the welcoming presence here. We let go of all challenges, hurts, frustrations, and disappointments. Here in the softness inside, in the welcoming presence is the warmth of our heart. Rest, let go, and breathe here. This warmth is love inside, it is the supreme love, it can heal any challenge, any fear, any doubt. Here disappointments melt in the radiant beam of unending love and acceptance. This flame, this truth is God Herself manifest in us as warm and nurturing.

The Mother shows us Her warmth in the center flame of our heart. Her love is our love. The flame grows brighter and larger. It spreads through our whole body, mind, all cells, in between every cell and melts everything that is no longer needed. We let go in the flame of love that purifies our being where only our diamond heart & mind remains.

Movement Meditation: I gather everything that is and bring it up through the center of my body, out the top of my head. Everything that is I AM.

Kali

Known as: Rhythm of Life & Eternity, Purifier of the blood of evil, Aligner of Souls Purpose

Experienced as:

All rhythms of nature, body, heavenly bodies. Freedom. Can be experienced as destruction or more accurately the dissolving of the material (mundane) world to release (free) the spirit.

Governs:

Directing our purpose in life. Our ability to move beyond the realm of Time. To gain perspective over the human condition. She is the Mother of Time which reveals Eternity. When we understand reincarnation, the cycle of birth and death, we are directed to find our purpose and why we are here. She cleanses the impurities of karma from our blood (human condition). She conquers incarnation.

Heart Meditation of Kali:

We let go of all holding. Holding onto wants or desires, we let go. Holding onto pictures of how things should be, we let go. Holding onto others we breathe and let go. Slowly, slowly we fall inward. Farther and farther inside, into an ocean of being. The waves flow in and out on the shore of life as we continue to let go even more.

Feeling the rhythm of the great ocean being pulled and pushed by the cycle of the moon we feel our own breath coming in and out. We are inside a living organism of nature and we surrender to its rhythm. We let go of all holding. Beyond this we are in the rhythm of time. Time carries the years of our life, body, our incarnation. Feeling this rhythm our awareness moves into eternity spreading out. My breath rises and falls effortlessly on timeless waves in the depth of the ocean inside.

The great Mother takes us by the hand showing us her sweetness, her guiding presence. She gives meaning and purpose to this life. We feel the sweet presence of peace as she guides our Souls. We radiate this peace to all beings. The deep night sky is our awareness greeting the All. My breath is peace, my heart is peace, Her heart is our peace.

Movement Meditation:

I am a wave. I flow with the rhythm of my own life. I flow with the rhythm of the moon and the stars. I am time itself, I am eternity.

Chinnamasta

Known as:

The transformer, the untangler of the karmic web, Vajra Yogini

Experienced as:

Paradigm shift, dissolving, letting go, untying, softening, non grasping, balance, equanimity, drinking directly from the heart, lightning.

Governs:

Thinking that the answers are outside of ourselves when the answers are found in our heart. She directs the focus of awareness to the heart as the source of the All. She cuts off her ego mind to focus only on the emanation of heart essence, God's love, the highest truth.

Heart Meditation of Chinnamasta:

We drop out of our heads and dive deep into the warmth of our hearts. Rest our awareness in the source of our being, our heart. We let go of finding answers in our mind or head and seek knowing in the heart. We hold our mind in loving hands and allow our awareness to drop into the warm source of love in our heart. This is life's essence. It is full and complete. All questions are told here, known here. All wisdom (the true blood of being) is alive here in every moment.

We receive the essence of our hearts, our true selves, the Love, the Source, the emanation of Divine goodness. We let this spread through your whole body and beyond our body to everyone and everything. The Source in our hearts sustains all life, it is the point of meditation; to receive your wisdom your soul as the Light of God.

Movement Meditation:

Holding the Light of God inside dissolves my attachments, my emotions, my ego and my thoughts, and I am becoming free.

Bagala

Known as:

Cuts our all untruth (the mundane) to reveal oneness; the pure reality, the Light & Love of God

Experienced as:

Self realization, oneness, the All in this moment, present moment expanding, still point within, discernment.

Governs:

Expansion of the heart which stops the outward focus of the mind (the tongue), which experiences separation from the soul, our hearts.

Heart Meditation of Bagala:

We rest our awareness inside and feel the welcoming invitation of our hearts. We let go and melt inside, letting go of all constricted thoughts or feelings. Feeling into the center of the center of our hearts and allow opening to enter. Feelings of being tight and small, hidden or self important begin to loosen as we enter a great landscape, the great gentleness within. Here there are open fields of kindness.

We drop inward into the very center of our hearts as if an arrow has carried us here directly. Holding the very center point of our heart steady we continue to expand from here. Feeling the pierce of the arrow in the center of our heart we let go. In the letting go expansion occurs and we expand farther and farther, inside our body and beyond our body. We feel the very center point of our being and the expansion of the heart at the same moment. We are standing in the ever expanding moment. This moment is all moments, timeless and borderless.

Movement Meditation: I am one with everything I see. I am one with everything unseen. As I open my arms I expand to the horizon. My mind is still and time stops.

Sundari

Known as:

The nectar of Heaven, Soma

Experienced as:

Grace, sweetness, tenderness, unending nourishment direct from Source, oneness with the Divine.

Governs:

The sweetness of our soul as the pure essence of God, nectar from our Spiritual Heart. The flow of God through our lives, being touched by God.

Heart Meditation of Sundari:

Taking a deep breath we exhale and let go of all sadness, all hopelessness, all fear. We breathe in and out in a natural rhythm and a softening occurs. We hold our human heart in all its tenderness and disappointments. We breathe and let go.

Here grace enters in the center of our being. We curl up inside the grace and it becomes a gentle rain of grace. This sacred rain moistens the hardened earth of the heart. We let go. Our bodies open like we can stretch out inside for the first time. Breathing in and out we receive the rain of pure love, pure care, pure serenity all over us and deep inside of us.

We stand in it like a waterfall, we swim in it as if it were a warm ocean lagoon with a white sandy bottom. All impurities are dissolved, all hurts are healed in the healing salve of grace.

Movement Meditation:

I gather all the sweet golden nectar that is falling from Heaven. It is constantly falling. It flows through my whole body and the bird of my heart (my soul) drinks from it.

Matangi

Known as:

The Mother River

Experienced as: A river, going with the flow of life, surrender, the All and Everything as a River, salvation

Governs:

The flow of consciousness through the body and God through our life. They are not two but one. The flow of our life is God. Experienced as surrender, service, enlightenment, humility.

Heart Meditation of Matangi:

Float inward into your heart. Flow deeper and deeper as if on a river inside. We let go of holding things as they were or how we want them to be. We are just flowing with the River of time. The river of divine carrying. The river lifts us and guides us perfectly in this moment. We cannot be anywhere else but in this flow, this point in our lives.

This river is the flow of our lives. It is the flow of God in our lives. We go with the flow of God through our body, mind and soul. We let go of all holding, all grasping. We let the river carry us to the ocean of God that awaits us, that is in us, that is us. We are all flowing down the river of life together.

Movement Meditation:

I am sitting with the Mother River. She is the giver of all life. I give everything back to her. I hold onto nothing. She washes me and takes everything from me.

GLOSSARY OF TERMS

Divine Mother: God as Mother, Para Shakti, Pure Spirit

Durga: Represents the Divine Mother who contains ten cosmic powers or Mother Goddesses within her, the Mahavidyas, who can interact with and influence all levels of matter throughout the Causal Realm, Astral and Physical Realms. She is also the Guru that the heart of the devotee merges with.

God: Source, All, Light, The One, Oneness, Spiritual Heart, Divine Mother/Father God, Creator, It, Alah, Yahweh, The Infinite, The All and Everything, Aliveness

Goddess: Enlightened beings that are different aspects of the Divine Mother.

Karma: The spiritual inheritance of past lives which is the collection of experiences and actions throughout lifetimes of existence that influence our behavior and determine the course of our current life.

Mahavidyas: Ten Wisdom Mothers, the ten goddesses of Yoga Tantra known as Dhumavati, Bhuvaneshwari (Mother Mary), Tara, Kamala (Lakshmi), Bhairavi, Kali, Chinnamasta, Bagala, Sundari, and Matangi.

Mind: Communication system and ego structure the Soul needs in Physical, Astral or Causal Planes.

Nirvana: Inner life, one with God, Samadhi

ParaShiva/ParaShakti: the all-pervasive pure consciousness, power, and primal substance of all that exists, God.

Realms (Physical, Astral, Causal): 3 Regions or planes (subtle state) of existence below the realm of Pure Spirit (God). The Causal Realm is the abode of Lord Siva and His entourage of Mahadevas and other highly evolved souls who exist in their own self-effulgent form or radiant bodies.

Samsara: The cycle of death and rebirth. Life energy focused on temporary existence.

Samadhi: Liberation from Samsara, awareness/soul merged in God while still being in the physical body.

Sanyasin: A person who dedicates their life to spiritual truths and pursuits.

Soul: Our soul, our spirit, is the direct Light of God, aliveness Itself, enlivening our bodies.

Vajra: Lightening force.

Vedas/Vedic Knowledge: The most ancient Hindu scriptures of India Believed to have been directly revealed to seers among the early Aryans in India, and preserved by oral tradition.

Vrittis: Agitations, waves or ripples of disturbance upon the otherwise calm waters of the Mind, caused by karma.

ABOUT THE AUTHOR

At age six, Ruth had a spiritual awakening in her first ballet class. Her heart burst open to the divine and joy filled her body. She felt she was dancing to God, as all and everything. Her dance became her devotional practice, which eventually matured into the energetic studies of Yoga, Chi Gung, Ayurveda and the movement of consciousness through the body and beyond the body.

Ruth began meditation practice at the age of 16 when she embraced Surat Shabd Yoga as her spiritual path. Ten years later she started visiting many holy sites in India including Punjab region, Rishikesh, Hardwar, Varanasi, and most recently Chennai. She is a continuing student of Vedic, Tantric wisdom & Mystic Catholicism, with particular connection to the teachings of Ramana Maharshi, the silent saint.

In 2005, she began an energetic study of the MahaVidyas, Wisdom Mothers of Yoga Tantra, while living and teaching in Assisi, Italy, the home of St Francis of Assisi. From this yearlong contemplation sprung a chi gung style movement practice that helps people embody spiritual teachings.

Concurrently she created a meditation dialogue sequence that guides people to experience their spiritual heart, the energetic core of our being that is one with the Absolute. This transformational work helps stabilize peace in our daily life.

Even though an avid seeker of the ultimate truth from a young age, she leads a householder's life. She raised two daughters (with two grandchildren) and has owned various restaurants. Business life, family life, and spiritual seeking have always been her world view. In 1993, after the death of her first husband, she committed to leading Heartfulness silent retreats with her current partner and husband, Bruce Davis. She holds certifications in Clinical Hypnotherapy & NLP.

In 2000, Ruth and her husband Bruce Davis founded the Assisi Retreat Center, a Temple to the World Religions in the heart of the ancient city of Assisi, Italy. In 2002, they created their first Silent Stay, converting an old farmhouse into a hermitage for guests to immerse themselves in the silence of their hearts.

In 2012, they founded Silent Stay Meditation Center in Vacaville, California. Having served over 2200 guests, a wildfire came through one fateful night in 2020 and burned the center to the ground along with 50 years of their spiritual collections.

But one thing remained..... the peace found in the silence, which can never be taken or destroyed. The center reappeared two years later in Santa Barbara, California and they began anew.

To find out more about Ruth's teachings see:

www.SilentStay.com
www.AssisiRetreats.org
www.TheMotherPractice.yoga

CPSIA information can be obtained
at www.ICGtesting.com
Printed in the USA
JSHW030928271222
35404JS00001B/96